The Summer of Mended Hearts

DEBBIE WALTZ

EABooks Publishing
Your Partner In Publishing

ISBN: 978-1-966382-65-2
LCCN: 2026901974

Cover design: Robin Black
Cover photos: man in wheelchair, EyeEm Mobile GmbH; young woman, VMStock; sunset sky, Prasit Supho

Published by EABooks Publishing, a division of
Living Parables of Central Florida, Inc. a 501c3
EABooksPublishing.com

Dedication

To my Mom and Dad,

> Thank you for being my sounding board, my editors, and my steady support. Your love, wisdom, and encouragement helped shape this book and carried me through every step of the journey.

To my Heavenly Father,

> You placed this idea in my heart and never let it go. Through quiet seasons and bursts of inspiration, you kept the flame alive. This book is my offering back to You, a reflection of Your faithfulness and grace.

To the Disabled Community,

> This book is for you. I hope these pages remind you that you are seen, known, and never alone. Your courage and resilience are a light to the world.

> *You know when I sit down and when I rise up;*
> *You discern my thoughts from afar* (Psalm 139:2).

CHAPTER 1

Swoosh.

An alert on Lisa's cell phone sounded, announcing a new text message. She had just gotten her phone back from her parents after being grounded for two weeks, and already there were over forty unread texts. But she was in no mood to read them. Probably just texts from her friends, sharing their excitement about summer plans. No, thank you. She swiped away the notification and refocused her attention on the candy-matching game she'd been playing.

Downstairs, her parents were fighting . . . again. She could hear them through the heating vent in the corner of her bedroom.

Yup, it was about her again.

As usual, their conversation had started civilly—they discussed their teenage daughter's moodiness and inability to complete simple chores without complaint. But also, as usual, it had quickly spiraled to them questioning each other's parenting skills.

There was some truth to what they said. Lately, she met even the simplest of questions with an annoyed glare. She really didn't want to act that way, and often she made promises to herself to change. But she couldn't help how she felt.

A message dropped from the top of her screen signaling she'd lost the level. She tossed the phone to the other side of the bed. No use anyway. Despite having heard this same argument a thousand times, she couldn't concentrate. She rolled onto her back, stretched her arms out across the pink quilt, and allowed her parents' voices to flood into the room.

"I don't know what to tell you, Marion. She's a teenager. Her behavior is pretty normal, all things considered."

That was just like her father, always sticking up for her, whether she deserved it or not.

"Defending her behavior isn't going to help. If she doesn't bring her grades up, she won't graduate next year."

"I know that . . . I know!" But you can't rush her grieving process. You can't expect her to get over everything on your schedule."

"Don't do that, Peter. Don't make me out to be the heartless one. I'm not. I know how hard it's been for her. For all of us. But I still expect her to make an effort."

"Yes, but grounding her and keeping her from her friends isn't helping. It's only made her more belligerent."

"What else can we do? Just give up on her and let her repeat the eleventh grade? At least I'm trying to do *something*."

"Compared to me, I guess, who's done nothing."

Lisa grabbed her cell phone from where it had landed by her pillow and quickly turned on her favorite playlist. She turned the volume up, hoping to drown out the sounds of her parents fighting, then tossed the phone back toward the pillows. She was so sick of this, and best she could tell, there was no end in sight.

Over the past months, the conflicts between the three of them had been building. They were all struggling to adjust to the new norm—one without Ryan. But how much longer could the family survive this sort of existence? And was that all they would ever have to look forward to again—just existing?

What would Ryan think if he could see them now?

Her brother's sweet face flooded her mind. His deep brown eyes, wild curly hair, dimpled cheeks, and ever-mischievous smile—how she missed him!

He was nine years old when they first noticed bruising on his body. He was playing Little League Baseball, and his mother assumed that was the cause. Later episodes of fatigue left him too tired to play, and he quit in late season. When he began complaining of constant leg pain and spent his days indoors, rather than playing with his friends, she took him to his pediatrician.

Shortly after, extensive blood work revealed an abnormal white blood count, and Dr. Andrews referred them to a pediatric oncologist at City Hospital. Within a month, Ryan was diagnosed with Acute Lymphocytic Leukemia and began treatment.

During Ryan's illness, the family had to make significant changes; Lisa's mother exchanged her busy realtor schedule and active role in Lisa's debate and swim teams for doctors' appointments, chemo treatments, and Ryan's frequent hospital stays. Her father took on additional landscaping work, taking whatever jobs he could—which meant taking jobs further and further from home. Then he spent evenings going door-to-door looking for more work.

Lisa, too, had changed a lot. She quit the debate and swim teams to pitch in at home, cleaning and cooking, and spending every spare minute she could with Ryan. One of her favorite things during those months was snuggling in bed with him to read C.S. Lewis books together, especially after one of his grueling treatments.

After over a year of aggressive chemotherapy treatments, Ryan was showing good results and entered remission. Through it all, he'd handled everything like a champ—the chemo treatments that left him vomiting and weak, and unable to eat, the painful spinal taps, the endless blood tests—he'd endured it all with little complaint. By spring, Ryan seemed to be regaining his strength. They were all so hopeful.

When the cancer returned, the following fall, Ryan began an even more intense series of treatments. But even stem cell transplants failed to stop the cancer's progression. The doctors offered no real hope for Ryan's recovery.

Ryan accepted the doctor's prognosis with strength and courage. Their parents eventually decided to bring him home so they could spend as much time with him as possible before the inevitable.

Lisa's mom arranged hospice for Ryan, which provided daily nurse visits to monitor his pain, regulate his medication, record vitals, and make him as comfortable as possible. They welcomed the support during his last days.

In mid-November, Ryan slipped away, with Lisa and her mom at his side. Her father was miles away in the next county, looking for a winter job. He never made it home to say goodbye.

The thought of that last night with Ryan was too much for Lisa. She grabbed her phone and opened her messaging app. Anything was better than those painful memories. With her parents' voices still echoing through the floor, she began clicking on her unread messages one at a time.

The first message she clicked on was from her best friend, Melissa. She and her family would soon cruise out of Baltimore to celebrate her parents' twentieth anniversary in the Caribbean. Next, her friend Katie wrote about her plans to spend July with her grandmother at her retirement condominium in Miami Beach.

With summer fast approaching, it seemed like all of Lisa's friends had special plans. It was their last summer before senior year and graduation, and many would be leaving home for college after the next school year ended. Both Melissa and Katie had already visited college campuses and would probably spend part of their summer preparing applications. Not Lisa. The only thing she faced this summer was a future of more tests, more schoolwork, more criticism, and the potential of more failure.

Lisa sat up and swung her legs over the edge of her bed. She had heard it all before, and it was true. Tears welled in her eyes. "I need to get out of here."

As if on cue, her cell phone chimed. She was in no state to talk to anyone. Probably another annoying marketing call anyway. Or worse, one of her friends calling to ask about her summer plans. She let it go to voicemail. She wiped the tears from her eyes, picked up her cell phone, and continued making her way through her text messages. She opened one from the library—a reminder about her overdue books. Lisa groaned. "That's probably where I'll be spending my summer."

Tossing the phone aside, Lisa threw herself back onto the bed. Old, condemning thoughts haunted her once again.

It wasn't always like this. They had been a normal family once. So happy . . . before Ryan got sick. Now it had all changed. Now she was an only child. Practically an orphan—her parents hated her. The only thing she brought to their lives anymore was a reason to fight and scream at each other. They were all in pain, but she was just making it worse with her terrible attitude and failing grades.

"Ugh! I hate this!" She stared through blurry eyes at her ceiling and tried to focus on the blades of her fan as they circled around and around. Squeezing her eyes tightly shut, she fought to hold back the overwhelming sadness—her constant companion since last fall—only to feel more warm tears trickle from the outer corners of her eyes.

Remember to stop and breathe. This was the advice her guidance counselor had given after she knocked on her office door in tears after being bullied by a group of girls. "It means you're still alive, and the bullies haven't won," she'd said.

That's right. She took a deep breath and welcomed the air back into her lungs. Yes, she still had her life to live. The negative words had no hold on her. She couldn't let them. Ryan would want her to live life to the fullest because he couldn't.

Lisa turned to her side and wiped her tears with the edge of her pink quilt, then searched for her phone amidst the now crumpled blankets and pillows. When she found it, there was a new voicemail. Scott's number. Clicking on the message, her excitement grew as she listened.

Hey, Lisa! It's Scott. I hope you're getting my messages. I know it's been a while. I'm sorry I haven't called sooner, but I've had a lot going on since we last talked.

There was a momentary pause before he continued.

I wish we could talk face to face. Is there any chance you'll be visiting your aunt this summer? I sure would love to see you. Give me a call, will you? Okay, well, I'll catch up with you later. Bye for now.

Lisa couldn't believe her ears. It had been nearly a year since she'd talked to Scott. He had called just after Uncle Frank died. Even now, his voice sent excited tingles down her spine.

The last time she saw him was two summers earlier, the last summer the whole family went to the farm. The McCarthys attended Ryan's funeral, but basketball season had started, and Scott had to be there—the team, and college scholarships were on the line. After Ryan's death their contact became limited to a few scattered texts and eventually turned to silence between them.

Lisa met Scott the summer her family visited her Aunt Jane and Uncle Frank, who had moved to a twenty-acre farm in rural Ohio. Scott had befriended her right away, a scrawny, pig-tailed tomboy. They spent much of that summer fishing at Thompson's Pond, climbing trees, and roaming the woods behind the farm.

Scott was twelve when they met, and Lisa was only ten. She was fascinated with his fearlessness from the very beginning. He didn't seem afraid of anything, and each summer, his boyish antics and mischief evolved. It was as if he were on one endless adventure. From his dangerous high jumps on the dirt bike and reckless free jumps from the upper loft in the barn into the hay piles below, to the summer he set off fireworks in the chicken coup. Even broken bones didn't deter him. Such a crazy guy! Always managing to get into some kind of trouble.

After the first two summer visits, Lisa and Ryan were allowed to spend several weeks of summer vacation with their aunt and uncle. The more time that Scott and Lisa spent together, the closer they grew; they shared their problems as well as their hopes and dreams for the future, often over double-scoops of ice cream at the local mom-and-pop grocery store.

Scott grew from a loud, reckless twelve-year-old into a more serious, committed young man. In high school, he became an outstanding student and successful athlete, and one of the most popular boys at his school. Scott had also changed physically. Summers of working on his parents' farm in the hot Ohio sun had turned his once ashy blonde hair almost golden. Hours of heavy barn work had developed his strong, muscular body, and his deep, sun-tanned face highlighted his gorgeous baby blue eyes.

The summer Lisa turned 13 she realized she felt a strange new attraction to him, and Lisa had her first crush on a boy.

Surely every girl dreamed of a guy like Scott—popular, athletic, kind, and extremely good-looking. But still a little wild. That was, after all, the trait Lisa had always found attractive.

Lisa stared at his voicemail and suppressed the urge to play it again. Had he changed much since the last time she saw him? Lisa smiled, suppressing a giggle. Although she was sure no one knew, she secretly hoped they might end up together one day.

Yeah, right. In your dreams!

Lisa laid her phone on the nightstand and curled up on her bed. She pulled one half of her bed quilt over her, and, before she knew it, she had drifted off to sleep, memories of Scott still spinning in her head.

CHAPTER 2

Still no reply from Lisa. Hopefully, everything was okay.

Nineteen-year-old Scott McCarthy flipped his old cell phone closed. He had been trying to contact her for several days with no luck. Now, he was getting worried. Although they hadn't spoken for some time, it wasn't like her to not respond to his calls or at least send a quick text.

They had been friends since the first day they met. Lisa and her family had been visiting the Mitchells, whose property backed up to his family's. Scott's mother suggested he do the neighborly thing and invite her over to see the horses and miniature goats and make her feel welcome. He'd agreed, begrudgingly, but to his surprise, he actually enjoyed her visit.

She'd been just a kid, but he'd allowed her to tag along with him and his pals the rest of the summer as they explored the woods and fields behind the farm. Each summer after, Lisa had invited herself to join them just about everywhere they went, tagging along on their adventures, whether trailing through the woods to their "hideaway" or heading down to the pond to skip rocks. Sometimes, Lisa brought her little brother, Ryan, along. It always slowed them down, but she insisted. At first, the guys found the whole arrangement irritating, but soon, they accepted her and little Ryan as part of their "summer gang."

Eventually, his friends began teasing Lisa about liking Scott, but she denied it emphatically, and soon, the teasing stopped. Despite the age difference and long time apart, a bond of friendship formed that seemed unbreakable.

Scott said a silent prayer. *Please, Lord, let our friendship survive this, too. I have a lot to tell her, and I hope she'll understand.*

A prayer like that would have never passed his lips a year ago, but a lot had changed since then. He'd been raised by Christian parents, attended church regularly, read his Bible, and knew all the rules for "living a godly life." He even followed them when it suited him. But now, things were different. Now he believed and lived his faith. Now he truly trusted that with God, he could thrive. Even now.

Lisa woke up to a knock on the bedroom door.

"Honey," her father said, "dinner is ready; come on down."

"Thanks, Dad, I'll be right there."

Lisa flung back the blanket, swung her legs over the edge of the bed, and stood. She had no idea how long she'd been asleep, but the sleep had temporarily lifted her bad spirits.

Standing at the sink in her bathroom, she peered into the mirror and studied the girl looking back at her. "Yikes!" Her curly chestnut brown hair lay matted against her face, and dark blue shadows encircled her puffy eyes. "What can I make of this mess?" she asked the reflection in the mirror. After washing her face, she applied a thin layer of soft peach lip-gloss and brushed her hair.

That would have to do.

After the dinner table was cleared, Lisa made her way into the kitchen. Her mother stood at the sink washing dishes. Lisa stood next to her.

"Mom?" she began, grabbing a dry towel and a clean plate to dry. "I've been thinking a lot about Aunt Jane lately. She must be lonely without Uncle Frank. I think it would be nice if I could visit her this summer." She stopped what she was doing and looked at her mother. When there was no response, she continued. "I think I could use the change, you know? I think you and Dad could, too."

Lisa went back to drying dishes and making neat stacks on the counter next to the sink. "So would that be okay with you and Dad? I know I'm just making things worse around here anyway."

"Absolutely not." Her mother dropped the fork she'd been washing back into the soapy water and stared at Lisa with a look of disbelief.

"But Mom—"

"No. End of discussion." She pulled the fork back out of the water and scrubbed it hard with the dishcloth. ""You have too much schoolwork to catch up on, young lady."

"Girls, *please.*"

Lisa turned toward her father's voice as he stepped into the kitchen doorway, his hands held in the air pleadingly. "Can't we try to have one evening together without fighting? What is it this time?"

"I was just telling your daughter there's no way she's going to her Aunt Jane's this summer". She dried her hands on a dishtowel, then turned from the sink and folded her arms over her chest. "She has too much studying and makeup work to complete if she's going to pass her junior year."

Her father's brow rose. "Oh, so I guess I have no say in this at all then."

It was hard for Lisa to hear her parents disagree. They had always made their decisions together. That all changed when Ryan became ill. With her father working longer hours to help cover medical expenses, often being gone for twelve to fourteen hours a day, it left her mother to make many of the medical decisions independently. It seemed like a necessary choice, but Lisa always wondered if wasn't really her dad's way of avoiding the realities of Ryan's illness.

"You're not saying you actually agree with her, are you?" Her mom dropped her arms to her sides.

"Not necessarily, but I certainly would like to be part of the discussion."

"Okay, so let's discuss it," Marion tossed the dishtowel next to the sink. "We'll give you our decision as soon as your father and I have discussed it," she said, then headed toward the doorway. Her father stepped aside to let her through, then turned and followed her to their bedroom.

On the last day of school, Lisa stood at her locker emptying books and papers into her backpack. With the locker empty, she slammed it shut for the final time this school year, then turned and joined the flood of students pouring down the hallways of Eastern High and spilling out the double front doors. On the other side of those doors, three months of freedom from books, teachers, and endless hours of sitting quietly in their seats, listening to teachers drone on about algorithms, US history, and the correct use of adverbs and adjectives awaited them. Well, most of them anyway.

Outside, a cool summer breeze, unusual for the Michigan summers, brushed Lisa's face and lifted her spirit. She closed her eyes briefly, inhaling the sounds and fresh air. Although she wasn't sure what awaited her this summer, she felt a sense of freedom. Summer would be what she made of it, and she still had high hopes it included a summer trip to Aunt Jane's.

"Lisa! Over here. Are you coming or what?"

Lisa scanned the line of cars in front of the school until she caught sight of her best friend, Melissa, her arms wildly waving over the dashboard of a shiny blue convertible. They'd agreed to meet after school. Two weeks grounded meant they had a lot of catching up to do.

Pulling alongside the high school's main entrance, Melissa grinned from ear to ear. Her vibrant red hair was pulled back into a ponytail and topped with a ragged University of Michigan Football cap, a gift from her brother, Luke, during his first year of college. One of the oldest girls in her class, she had gotten her driver's license before most of her classmates. And she was never afraid to show it off.

"Nice ride. Where did you get it?" Lisa opened the passenger door and slid inside.

"It's Luke's. He let me borrow it for the last day of school." Melissa chuckled. "Guess he finally trusts me not to wreck it." She ran her fingertips across the smooth leather interior. "Maybe I'll have one just like it someday."

"Maybe," Lisa said half-heartedly, a little jealous of her friend.

"Hey, girlfriend." Melissa's eyebrows pulled together. "What's up? Talk to me."

Lisa shrugged and fiddled with the buckle on her purse. Where to begin? There were so many things, really. For one, several weeks had passed since she'd asked her parents about going to her aunt's, and they still hadn't given her an answer. The waiting was unbearable and probably meant the answer was a big fat "no." As far as everything else . . . none of it was something she really wanted to talk about—even with her best friend. Still, it was no surprise she hadn't been able to fool her. Melissa always knew when something was bothering her.

The two first met in the second grade when Lisa transferred into the Big Rapids School District. Being a shy child, she didn't make friends easily. Melissa, on the other hand, was well liked and outgoing. She approached Lisa sitting alone on the playground one day shortly after her arrival and immediately befriended her. Ever since that day, Melissa had always been there for her. In high school, when she became the victim of pranks and teasing because of the way she dressed in bold and vibrant mismatched colors, Melissa was her greatest defender. That year, their lockers were next to each other, so she stayed on the lookout for the harassing group, giving Lisa enough time to slip off to the girls' room or around the corner whenever they were coming. When the coast was clear, she would find her to let her know.

Melissa had also been her strongest support during Ryan's illness and by her side during Ryan's final days. She wouldn't have made it through those days and weeks without her—days and weeks that seemed to pass both too slowly and too quickly.

"Sorry." Lisa forced a smile onto her face, then looked her friend in the eyes. "It's nothing. I'm just really distracted today."

Melissa held her gaze. "No problem." She wasn't fooled, but just like she always knew when something was wrong, Melissa also knew when to give her space. She flipped the radio to her favorite station, and then pulled away from the curb.

At the Sanchez's, Melissa pulled into the driveway and put the car in the park. Lisa once again forced a smile.

"Thanks for the ride."

"Look." Melissa shifted toward her in the driver's seat. "I know you're still upset about failing Algebra but look on the bright side—at least you have summer to look forward to. We're going to have so much fun. Watch. Your parents will chill out soon, and things will get better. I'm sure of it."

"The jury's still out on that one."

Melissa tilted her head to the side. "What's that supposed to mean?"

"Oh, nothing. My parents just think I should spend the summer studying." Well, that was partly true at least. Maybe it was time to tell the whole truth. If she couldn't trust Melissa with it, whom could she trust?

"Actually, the truth is, I didn't just flunk Algebra. I flunked Chemistry, too, and I still haven't completed some other classes."

Melissa's mouth dropped. "Oh, no, Lisa. What are you going to do?"

"I really don't know. Honestly, I hardly even care right now. I've asked my parents to let me visit Aunt Jane this summer . . . it's like . . . I just feel like I need to get away and figure things out. They haven't given me an answer yet, but you know them; they'll probably say no."

"Hey, stop." She placed her hand over Lisa's. "Listen, I know your parents have been hard on you lately. Well . . . your mom at least." She smiled. "But they only want to see you succeed. Try to give them a break, will ya? You've all been through a lot."

Lisa pulled her hand away. "Give them a break? Are you serious? Why can't they give me a break!" She shook her head. "I just can't do it anymore, Melissa, I can't . . ." Tears warmed her eyes and blurred her vision. "Don't they get it? I can't be their perfect child. Their perfect child is dead!"

The words cut like a knife, but it was true. Finally, she'd said what she'd been feeling all along. Ryan had always been the perfect child. He never got in trouble, never caused their parents any heartache. The problem was her. It had always been her. This past year had just proven it.

"Lisa, no. I didn't mean it like that. All I mean is that . . . they're still grieving too. As hard as this is for you, just imagine how hard it is for them. Ryan was their *son*."

Melissa was right. She was. But she wasn't ready to admit it to anyone. She wasn't ready to think outside of her own pain. It just hurt too much. Ryan was gone, and nothing would ever be the same.

"Your parents do love you, Lisa. They just may not know how to show it right now. But things will get better."

Lisa stared out the window. "Go ahead; say it. You know you want to."

As long as she'd known Melissa, she'd been "religious." Her family went to church every Sunday and even invited the Sanchezes sometimes. But her friend being a "Christian" had never been a problem in the past. As friends, they understood and respected each other for their differences and left it at that. But something had changed during this school year—Melissa suddenly became bolder in sharing her beliefs, and sometimes, she just didn't want to hear it.

"I will then." Melissa again reached for Lisa's hand and squeezed it. "My family and I are praying for you. I know you'll find the strength you need to get through this, and life will get better."

"Right." She reached around the back of her seat and grabbed her backpack." Thanks, again for the ride."

"Listen, I'm sorry if I'm being pushy. You know me; I say what I think. It's just that something tells me God is going to show Himself to you this summer."

"Show Himself?" Lisa dropped her bag on her lap and glared at her friend. A flush of anger rushed into her face. "A little late for that, don't you think? He could have saved my little brother and helped me believe at the same time. Why didn't He show himself then?"

"I don't know, Lisa. We aren't always given the answers, but—"

Lisa held up her hand to stop Melissa, then shoved the passenger door open and slipped out in one motion. Without a word, she slammed the car door behind her, and then stormed up the porch steps to her house and inside.

She had heard the story from Melissa before and at the church they attended when she was younger. But the idea of a merciful God just sitting back and letting terrible things happen didn't make sense. Where was the love and mercy of God they all talked about? No, she had every right to be angry. Any God who would do that to her family didn't deserve her trust or her love.

And nothing—absolutely nothing—was gonna change that.

Lisa was still in her pajamas and in bed, at ten a.m. Saturday morning, thumbing through a fashion magazine, when her mother called her.

"Lisa! Please come down here. We need to talk to you."

Had they finally come to a decision about Aunt June's? Or was that being too hopeful? Maybe they were going to tell her they were getting a divorce. Her stomach twisted and tightened at the thought. Despite how terrible things had been since Ryan's death, living angry together had to be better than living apart, or divorced.

She found both of her parents in the living room waiting for her. They sat on opposite ends of the sofa. When she entered the room, her mom motioned toward the loveseat across from them. She lowered herself slowly into the seat, in no rush to hear what was coming. Living room discussions were always so serious. And they never ended well.

Her mother began hesitantly, as if searching for the right words. "You've probably noticed us acting rather . . . badly lately."

She stifled a nervous laugh. Badly? She couldn't remember a day in the past several months that they weren't fighting or not speaking to each other at all.

"Are you getting a divorce?"

There. She'd said it.

Her mom shot a sympathetic look at her father. "Frankly, Lisa, we have discussed the possibility, but neither I nor your dad want that. We realize things have been quite difficult for all of us since Ryan died, and then Uncle Frank, but we want to work things out."

Her father leaned forward, resting his elbows on his knees, and looked her in the eyes. "Lisa, you deserve two parents who aren't fighting all the time."

Her mother nodded. "But if that's going to happen, we can't continue like this. So, we talked with your aunt, and we agree; your visiting the farm might be the best thing right now. For all of us. But there are conditions."

And there it was. There was always a "but."

"I've spoken to your teachers and arranged for you to do summer makeup work for the two incomplete classes, and when you return from your aunt's, you'll retake your final exams in Algebra and Chemistry. This means you'll have to focus on your studies while you're there."

"You should consider yourself very lucky." Her father clasped his hands between his knees. "The school has taken your circumstances into consideration, but they didn't have to. I hope you won't take this opportunity for granted. Your Aunt Jane will monitor your schoolwork and report back to us. You can leave Monday morning. I'll get the truck ready for you."

Ordinarily, Lisa would have been ecstatic; she was going to Aunt Jane's for the summer. But her enthusiasm was dampened by the "conditions" laid down. Not to mention, the thought of what might happen between her parents while she was away. Sure, they seemed okay now, but she had seen too much these months to think that their current bright outlook would last. Still, the conversation could have gone a lot worse. And, after all, wasn't this what she'd wanted?

CHAPTER 3

Monday morning, Lisa woke at dawn. Sleep hadn't come easily, and her dreams had left her uneasy. Even now, almost two years after Ryan's death, thoughts and memories of him followed her during the day, and dreams interrupted her peaceful sleep at night. This morning was worse than usual.

Perhaps it was because she was going to Aunt Jane's—she hadn't been there since his remission, and it was a place full of wonderful memories for her and her baby brother.

Oh, dear sweet Ryan! If only you were here, we could be a happy family again.

As hard as Lisa tried, she couldn't erase the memories of those first weeks after Ryan's death. She could still hear her parents crying through her bedroom wall, as she lay sleepless in her bed at night. And her mother sobbing behind the locked door of Ryan's bedroom during the day. But worse of all may have been hearing her father, the man she'd always been able to count on for strength, sound so completely broken. His words often replayed themselves in her mind.

Why did God take our little boy? Why? Isn't God supposed to be a loving Father? How could a loving father do this?

Hearing her father's turmoil played out wore on her. She couldn't tell from one second to the next whether he blamed God or doubted His existence entirely. Maybe he didn't even know. Or maybe it just helped him, having someone to blame. Maybe the guilt of not being there to say goodbye to his son was too much for him to bear.

The Sanchez family had never been religious, although her father was raised in a Catholic home with his grandmother. He recounted being brought up with countless warnings about God's existence but said that they felt more like tools used to keep him in line than anything. Warnings like, *God is watching you* and *you'd better be a good boy, or else.* Apparently, the picture of

God he'd been given was grounded more in a God who punishes the disobedient than in a loving Father.

When they first moved into their new home in Big Rapids, they attended a small evangelical church in their neighborhood, hoping to get better acquainted with the community and make new friends. They stopped attending after only a few months, though, except for the occasional holiday, like Christmas and Easter. It didn't help that her mother's job as a realtor often required her to work on Sundays, and her dad refused to go without her.

Lisa's eyes glistened, and a tear slipped from the corner of her eye. She swiped it quickly, biting the corner of her lip. She could never forget Ryan, but as painful as it was, it was time to move on. It's what Ryan would want. He was gone now; he would want her to get back on track. It was time to pack for the summer.

As she packed, she dismissed each memory of Ryan as quickly as it appeared, redirecting her focus to the opening and closing of her dresser drawers and shoving clothes to the side as she sorted out her favorite outfits. She picked out her favorite blue sweater, her best "go-to" blouses, several pairs of blue jeans, sweatshirts, her favorite blue denim skirt, and lots of socks and other necessities, and stuffed them all into her pink checkered suitcase next to the toiletries she'd already packed. As she pulled open her bottom dresser drawer to retrieve her favorite nightgowns, she stopped suddenly. There, tucked amongst her clothes, lay the tiny pink coin purse Ryan had given her for Christmas the year before he died. He had saved every penny he could that year to buy it for her. It had a special slot for her ID, a zippered coin pouch, and was covered in kisses. She glided her fingers across a tiny kiss, and on an impulse, picked it up and slipped it into the corner of her suitcase. Sighing, she slammed the drawer shut and moved on to her closet.

Lisa was surprised by her uplifted spirit. Something was changing in her attitude, and she was beginning to feel some of the negativity fading. Something felt different. Of course, she was excited about getting away, but there was something more. Over the past few days, she'd continued to be haunted by Melissa's prediction for the summer. Was she right?

Hope. Perhaps there is some hope.

Satisfied with her selections, she placed the last of her clothing items in her suitcase and zipped it up. As she picked up her backpack and tossed it on the bed next to the suitcase, she caught a glimpse of Mr. and Mrs. Wilson through her open bedroom window, walking down the sidewalk together. The Wilsons were the retired couple who lived in the white two-story house on the corner, two doors down. Lisa often saw them walking together, laughing, and sometimes holding hands, and every time she felt a pang of regret. She wished her parents could be like that . . . like they used to be.

Like Melissa's family, the Wilsons, too, were religious; she caught sight of them out the window most Sunday mornings, all dressed up and headed to church. Perhaps that was why they had been so supportive during Ryan's illness—Mrs. Wilson had cooked dozens of meals for them during the weeks Ryan was in the hospital, and Mr. Wilson kept the lawn nicely mowed and brought in the trash cans when Dad had forgotten to get them.

Turning back to her packing, Lisa picked up her laptop and stuck it in her backpack where her schoolbooks had already been packed, then quickly zipped the bag. She needed to get moving; Aunt Jane would be worried if she weren't off the road by dark, and she still needed to stop by Melissa's before she hit the highway. She stopped to view her room one last time; it would be a long while before she saw it again. For a teenager, her room was rather austere, with only a few school pictures and vacation souvenirs stuck on the wall. The top of her small pink desk was arranged with a stack of lined notepads, a pink flowered pencil holder filled with assorted pens, two schoolbooks she wouldn't need over the summer, and a small photograph of Ryan. It was from a beautiful day in early spring, before Ryan got sick again, and the family had decided to take a short trip to the Muskegon River. She and Ryan had spent the day fishing, skipping rocks, and sitting on the shore, talking and laughing. It was only a few months later that Ryan's cancer returned.

Stop it, Lisa!

She had to stop doing this to herself. She quickly slung her backpack over her shoulder, picked up her overstuffed suitcase, then lugged her load through the bedroom door, looking like a bellhop making his way through the lobby of a hotel. "Let's get this show on the road."

It was almost ten a.m. by the time she made her way downstairs to leave. Her parents had already had their first argument, and her dad had headed off to sulk in the garage—so much for their resolution to "make it work."

Downstairs, she looked for her mother first in the kitchen. However, she found only an empty coffee cup on the kitchen table and a sink of dirty dishes. She found her on the red plaid sofa in the family room, a fleece blanket tossed over her legs. Her eyes were closed, and she was still in her nightgown and wrinkled cotton bathrobe. She could wake her, give her a hug and tell her she'd miss her . . . but there was such a look of peace on her face as she slept, a look she hadn't seen in so long. No, she would call her once she got to Aunt Jane's instead. Returning to the kitchen, she grabbed a glazed donut from an open box on the counter.

A moment later, the sound of a sniffle came from the family room.

"Goodbye, honey, I love you."

"I love you too, Mom," Lisa said, then she shot out the kitchen's back door and into the garage.

As expected, Lisa found her father working underneath his beloved 1957 classic red convertible with big fins; the car took more than its share of space in the garage. The car had become part therapy, part escape since her brother's death, and it seemed to her he'd never finish fixing it up. Maybe that was by design. There was a time she'd been excited to drive it one day, but she'd given up on that hope long ago. While the car's exterior looked almost perfect, on closer examination, evidence of damage was unmistakable—a rusted and unstable frame and a burnt-out engine in need of a complete overhaul. Just like her family. Looked fine to the neighbors, but a corroded mess beneath the surface.

"Hey, Dad, I'm on my way out. I just wanted to say goodbye."

"Wait, you're going to need these." He pulled himself out from under the car, then reached into his pocket and pulled out a set of keys. He slid them across the floor toward her.

"Oh yeah, I will." She reached down and grabbed the keys. "Thanks, Dad. I love you."

"Love you too. Make sure you call us when you get there." He smiled, then slipped back under the car.

She exited the open garage door and walked toward the old 1985 4x4. Her dad had washed the light-blue pickup, but the dingy rust spots along the bottom stood out. It looked beat-up and not what a girl wanted to be seen driving, but it was transportation, and it would get her to Aunt Jane's. She dumped her load into the passenger's seat before rounding the back and climbing into the driver's side. With a turn of the key, she started the engine, cautiously backed down the driveway and onto the street, then gave the horn a quick tap to say goodbye.

So, it was a rusty old pickup—it was gonna get her outta there!

"Hey, Lisa. I'll take those from you." Melissa stood in her open front doorway and reached for the five library books Lisa held in her arms.

"Thanks for returning them for me," Lisa said. She was glad to see her friend didn't seem to be harboring any hard feelings after their last talk.

"Sure. I hope you have a wonderful time at your aunt's." She smiled brightly. "Well, I . . ." Melissa brushed a strand of hair behind her ear. "I, uh . . ."

Well, this was a first. Lisa had never, ever seen Melissa stammer. She always knew what to say.

Oh no, she's going to get all mushy now, isn't she?

Without warning, Melissa dropped the books to the floor and stepped outside onto the concrete porch.

"Well . . . I want you to know I'm gonna miss you." She reached out and pulled Lisa into a tight hug. "I think you are terrific, and I wish I could help more. I'm serious when I say I'm praying for you. I know God loves you."

It was nice—really nice—being hugged by Melissa. And it was genuine.

They said their goodbyes, then Lisa walked back to the truck, a smile spread across her face. As she turned the ignition, Melissa's mother called out to her from the front door.

"Lisa!" Mrs. Brumbaugh slipped around Melissa still standing in the doorway, then moved quickly down the porch steps and to the truck door. Lisa leaned forward and rolled down the window.

Mrs. Brumbaugh held up a wrinkled brown envelope, "We found this old Vacation Bible School packet of things Ryan made in class." She handed it to Lisa through the window. "He must have left them in Bobby's room. We wanted to give them to you and your family."

Lisa looked down at the package now clutched in her hand. Ryan's name was scribbled in red crayon on the outside of the envelope. A flood of emotion rose inside of her, threatening the peace she had just felt a moment before. She pulled open the glovebox and pushed the envelope inside. "Thank you, Mrs. Brumbaugh." She forced a smile to her lips, then shifted the truck into reverse and waved goodbye to Melissa and her mother as she slid out of the driveway.

CHAPTER 4

It was already past noon, and she still had a long drive ahead. Using the phone's GPS, she left her hometown behind and entered the freeway, gliding smoothly into the traffic, just as her pudgy driving instructor, Mr. Merkle, had taught her to do: *Gently, gently, get up to speed, and slip into traffic.* The memory of him holding onto the edge of the passenger's door with a death grip made Lisa smile.

After driving for over an hour, Lisa saw a sign for the next turnpike plaza, only nine miles ahead, advertising a pizza place and fast food burger restaurant. Her stomach gurgled, reminding her she had missed lunch. She took the exit and turned into the parking lot.

The plaza wasn't too busy. She approached the Burger King counter, ordered a burger and fries, and took the tray of food to a table near the window. While she ate, she looked around at all the people moving about their day. She suddenly felt as if she had achieved adulthood, making this trip all on her own. Her food finished, she wadded up her burger wrapper and tossed it, along with the rest of her trash, into the nearby can, then headed to the coffee kiosk. A nice hot cup of mocha peppermint coffee would be just what she needed for the rest of the ride.

Out in the parking lot, the sun felt good on her face. She hopped back into the blue pick-up and slid her coffee into the pull-out cupholder. "Let's get on the road, Bluebelle." She turned the key to start the engine. "Bluebelle . . . that's an appropriate name, my trusty old truck. We have a couple more hours, so I need you to stay focused and help me follow my phone directions. I'm counting on you to get me to Aunt Jane's."

By late afternoon, the fresh country air, clear blue sky, and lush fields of yellow sunflowers were helping her forget the problems she'd left behind. Everything seemed easier here; she could breathe more easily, and the dark clouds hanging over her head faded away. In just a short time, she would be with her aunt. She couldn't explain it, but even as a child, the connection between her and her aunt was special. She had always been able to talk to her aunt about boys, about the "mean girls" at school, and about Ryan—especially about Ryan. She shared her fears about Ryan's illness, and Aunt Jane always seemed to have a way of easing her fears and giving her hope.

Aunt Jane also had a free spirit. A flower child of the 1970s, she still wore her ankle-length maxi skirts and loose bohemian blouses, and her straight, gray, shoulder-length hair, simply cut to frame her delicate facial features, flipped softly in the back. She seemed to understand her and had always allowed her to be herself, to run around in jeans, climb trees, and roam the woods with the boys.

It would be good to be with Aunt Jane. She must have been lonely since Uncle Frank died, and it was past time for them to reconnect. Maybe over lunch at one of those Amish restaurants—oh, their food was good!—then shopping in those quaint little shops in town. They could go on drives through the country and have long talks like they used to. The more Lisa thought about it, the more excited she got.

The roads became narrower, with fewer houses along the way and farms sprinkling the landscape with tall, white silos, red barns, and Black Angus cows grazing on stacks of hay. Now and then, she saw a small house set far off the road with clotheslines peppered with black and white clothing, generally indicating an Amish-owned home. At one point, she carefully passed an Amish couple in a horse and buggy, and they gave her a friendly wave.

It was then that it hit her—she'd been so focused on her preparations for the trip that she had forgotten about Scott. She'd not even told him she was coming! How would he react to her surprise visit? She could wait until she got to Aunt Jane's, but with all the excitement of arrival and getting settled, she might forget, and then it would be too late at night to call. She pulled to the side of the road at an abandoned fruit stand and reached for her cell phone.

As her fingers hovered over her cell, doubt suddenly crept in. Should she just text him? It would be simpler and less awkward. She had not talked to him in almost a year, not since Uncle Frank died. Maybe she should just call and break the ice. After all, he had left a voicemail she never returned. What must he be thinking about her silence? In any case, she needed to thank him for giving her the idea of visiting Aunt Jane's in the first place and let him know she was on her way.

She debated for a moment more before finding his name in her contact list and calling.

Scott answered after several rings. After an uncomfortable greeting and a few moments of silence, she told him she would be in town later this evening. He said he was excited, and they made plans to meet in the next few days. But something in his voice made her feel uneasy. Hesitant, even.

"Oh, by the way. We don't live on the farm now. I'll text you our new address." Scott said just before hanging up.

Gone was the smooth and confident voice she used to know. Maybe he hadn't been looking forward to seeing her at all. Or perhaps it was something else entirely that had made him call a few weeks before. Guilt over his not checking in on her after Ryan's death? She'd wanted to tell him none of that mattered, but the whole conversation was just so strange that she had hurried to end the call as soon as she could. Had they lost their special connection? It sure hadn't sounded like it in his voicemail, but a lot of time had passed since they last saw each other. Maybe she was just overthinking it.

Well, there was nothing she could do about that now. She checked the mirror, then pulled back onto the long stretch of country highway, hoping things would be better between her and Scott once they were face-to-face.

Scott slapped his forehead. Could he have possibly been more awkward? Probably not, but he hadn't been prepared to hear her voice. Doubts flooded his mind. Maybe he wasn't ready to see her again. If only he'd given her some idea of what to expect. Too late to turn back now, though. She'd be at her aunt's farm in no time.

Scott closed his eyes and shifted his thoughts to Ryan, the bright, precocious little boy who loved adventures and exploring. All those summers he'd followed Lisa and him around like a puppy dog through the woods, climbing up every tree that he could manage. When Ryan wasn't with his sister and friends he was in his treehouse, reading or playing on his tablet. It was a cozy little structure, nestled in the limbs of the hundred-year-old oak tree just behind their barn. A five-by-five structure, but exactly right for Ryan, and built with recycled old lumber from an outbuilding his uncle had torn down. One of the window openings gave Ryan a great view of the hills beyond and the pond on the nearby property where Lisa and Scott often went to fish.

Uncle Frank tore the whole thing down a few days after Ryan's funeral.

Lord, Lisa and her family have been through so much, the grief and pain. Please comfort them as they continue to work through their grief and face life without Ryan and Frank. Lord, please lead and guide me if I can help her while she is here this summer.

Since Ryan's death, the idea of coming back to Aunt Jane's had been too painful. Aunt Jane's house was a tangible reminder of the happy family they had been and would never be again—not without Ryan and Uncle Frank. But it was time now, and she was ready.

Within a short time, Lisa found herself on the rural county road where Aunt Jane lived. The rays of sunset through a puff of cumulus clouds seemed to welcome her with open arms. It was as if she were going home—to her little hideaway in the country—at least for a little while. Here, she'd be able to find relief from the troubles at home. Aunt Jane's was someplace where she could temporarily set aside her failures, conflicts, and loneliness and find peace and comfort. It was one place where she wouldn't feel pressured and controlled, pulled in so many directions. For a little while, she could just be herself.

A smile crossed her face as she moved down the road. She passed the old grain mill, with its twin white silos, and then the little mom-and-pop store, where she and Ryan had so many times bought glass bottles of soda out of an antique ice chest. Outside a single old-fashioned gas pump stood beneath the shadow of an antique Texaco sign.

She passed the old trestle railroad bridge that ran high above the road. She remembered when Scott had walked across the rails on a dare and laughed at his friends who cringed in fear when he pretended to stumble. No one really thought it was so funny, but that was Scott. Memories surfaced, too, of the train's horn blowing in the night as it passed over the bridge while she lay near sleep in the cozy attic bedroom at Aunt Jane's house.

"We are almost there, Bluebelle!" Lisa's heart nearly leapt out of her chest with excitement.

She turned at the mailbox, shaped like a birdhouse, bright blue with a yellow roof, with the name "Mitchell" hand-painted across the side. Uncle Frank had made it for Aunt Jane for her birthday, the first year they lived on the farm. Everyone knew Jane Mitchell loved birds; it had been a passion of hers since childhood. Her home was filled with colorful books about birds, photos she had taken while bird watching hung on the walls, and the trees outside were filled with nearly a dozen bird feeders.

Lisa drove the pick-up slowly down the narrow gravel drive and past a clump of evergreens. And then it appeared. The modest two-story yellow house with its white front porch had not changed much since her last visit. The pink window boxes still overflowed with peonies and lavender, and masses of daffodils and tulips filled the flowerbeds at both corners of the house.

"It's so good to be home." And that was exactly how it felt. Like home.

Lisa pulled Bluebelle onto the grass on the far side of two cars that were already parked beside the house. One, she recognized as her aunt's—a pretty little red coupe. A surprise from her husband on her fortieth birthday. Aunt Jane had driven it for as long as Lisa could remember. But the other vehicle was unfamiliar, a deep-blue sports car that looked brand new. Did Aunt Jane have company?

Looking out the windshield, she could see the back of the old barn and spotted the old oak tree—yes, Ryan's treehouse was gone, just like her mom had said. Lisa sighed, then grabbed her backpack from the passenger seat, shut the truck off, and hopped out. Leaning against the driver's door, she looked around, deeply inhaling the fresh country air. As her eyes followed the green hills rising in the distance, a smile briefly touched her lips. Ryan had once called the largest of the hills "Mount Goofy," its mounding contour reminding him of one of his favorite Disney characters.

Lisa pulled her attention back toward the house. Truth was, she had expected her aunt to come bursting out the side porch door full of excitement by now, just as she and Uncle Frank had done on so many previous visits. But to her disappointment, she had not. Was this just one of the ways things would be different now that Uncle Frank was gone? She sure would miss the big bear hugs he gave. And sitting around the table as he shared stories of their first years on the farm. Like the time Aunt Jane planted potatoes in the garden with the roots from the eyes sprouting up from the ground. Uncle Frank said it looked like a herd of reindeer had been buried there with only their antlers above ground. How they had laughed about that. There was nothing like sitting on the front porch on warm summer nights while Aunt Jane and Uncle Frank reminisced about the "good old days." But that wouldn't happen this summer. Or ever again, for that matter.

Frank and Jane Mitchell had seen their share of hard times during their thirty years of marriage. They had experienced deep disappointment and heartbreak at their inability to have children. Both had dreamed of a big family.

Life on a farm could be difficult, and they'd had to endure financial problems as well. But neither seemed to mind. When Frank had taken a bad fall from the tractor and broken his right arm, Jane not only cheerfully took care of him, but also did what chores she could, and insisted the rest of them could just wait. Through it all, their love remained steady and strong. When asked how they remained so happy and content, even through life's disappointments, they always said, "That's God's doing, not ours."

It had been just a year since Frank died of a massive heart attack. In less than two years, Jane had lost not only her nephew but also her husband and best friend. And all the wishing in the world from their loved ones couldn't bring them back.

"Where is she?" Lisa whispered to herself. She must have seen her outside by now. Lisa pulled out her phone and checked the time. Yes, she was a bit earlier than she'd expected, but still . . .

Just then, laughter erupted from the house. Lisa hadn't heard Aunt Jane laugh like that in years. But the sound was unmistakable—without a doubt, that was Aunt Jane's uproarious laughter.

Well, that was enough standing around. Lisa walked around Bluebelle, past the gleaming blue sports car. She stopped to inspect the vehicle—a convertible polished to a shine. The license plate read "MYFAST55."

So, maybe it *wasn't* one of the church ladies.

Lisa put aside her disappointment at not being greeted and continued down the walkway to the back porch while enjoying the fresh smell of flowers all around. But nothing could have prepared her for what she would see as she stepped onto the porch and peered in through the kitchen screen door: Aunt Jane standing in the kitchen . . . in the embrace of a man! Her arms were wrapped around his neck, and she was touching his salt and pepper hair.

CHAPTER 5

"Aunt Jane?" Lisa glared through the kitchen screen door in shock.

Startled, Jane stepped back from the man, a rosy blush flooding her cheeks. "Lisa, sweetheart, you're here. I'm so happy to see you. Come on in, honey."

Lisa didn't move.

"Well, don't just stand there! Come on in." Her aunt motioned her inside. Finally, Lisa pushed open the door and stepped inside.

"Lisa, I'd like you to meet my friend, Mike," Aunt Jane said, still visibly flustered. "Mike, this is my niece, Lisa. I told you about her."

"Hey." Lisa's throat felt dry, and she did her best to avoid making eye contact with her aunt or the stranger, who said hello, then quietly took a step back from her aunt. "I'm just gonna take my things upstairs." Lisa maneuvered past them through the kitchen and toward the narrow staircase at the far side of the room.

"Lisa, please, I'd appreciate it if . . ." Aunt Jane's words fell on deaf ears as Lisa stomped up the stairs. It wasn't until she reached the guest room and slammed the door behind her that she realized she'd left her suitcase in the truck. Suddenly, her dramatic demonstration of disapproval left her feeling silly and embarrassed.

"Well, that was certainly a big surprise," she said to no one as she plopped on the edge of the bed. She turned her gaze toward the window. So Aunt Jane had a boyfriend. She couldn't believe it. How . . . why? Why would she want to do that? It made no sense.

She fell back against the soft mattress and stared up at the ceiling. Nothing, not the familiarity of the guest room and the handmade blue-and-yellow quilt beneath her, the white-painted antique dresser with the hand-embroidered runner, or the old rocking chair she used to sit in to read Ryan bedtime stories—none of these brought her comfort.

Everything was spoiled.

Her expectations of a summer alone with Aunt Jane had quickly faded. She had longed for their long talks over homemade apple pie even more than she'd realized now that the chance of them was gone. This new turn of events—this *man*—had changed everything.

She wanted to cry—and to scream! This was not how things were supposed to be. This wasn't what she'd wanted. It wasn't what she'd begged her parents for. Maybe she should have just listened to her mother and stayed home.

A car engine started outside. She jumped up and quickly moved to the window, pushing the sheer curtain aside to peek between the blinds. The blue sports car was slowly backing down the drive.

Betrayed.

Yep, that's how she felt. Betrayed. And yet, even as the word twisted and twirled around in her mind, fueling the feeling of anger inside, there was a part of her that understood how selfish she was being. But . . . still.

What was she going to do now? Aunt Jane was probably furious with her. Ugh! Why did she do the things she did? Why did she always let her emotions rule over her? She'd ruined the whole summer, and even if she could fix it, she didn't want to. She had wanted to spend the summer with Aunt Jane, not Aunt Jane and . . . *Mike.* Every cell in her body screamed for her to run downstairs and drive straight home, but she couldn't. She knew she couldn't.

Lisa settled into the old, familiar rocking chair, with its pink and blue, polka-dotted cushion, listening for sounds downstairs. Everything was quiet. She'd have to go down to the truck to get her suitcase eventually. Oh, how would she ever face Aunt Jane again?

She sat quietly in the chair and rocked for some time, quickly at first, but eventually her pace began to slow. In the quiet, dimly lit room, the exhaustion of the drive set in, and Lisa nearly slumped over the arm of the chair as she began to doze off. Shaking off her drowsiness, she reached for her backpack, pulled out her cell phone, and checked her messages.

Nothing from Mom and Dad yet. She'd better text them and tell them she arrived so they wouldn't worry.

What would she say?

She sent off a brief text, deciding to avoid the mention of anything about Aunt Jane's new friend.

This is ridiculous.

Like it or not, she was going to have to make this work somehow.

"Lisa, may I come in?" Jane asked, gently tapping on the bedroom door.

After a moment, Lisa responded in a resolute voice. "It's your house."

Aunt Jane opened the door and stepped inside. Lisa looked up from the rocking chair.

"I just wanted to apologize. I know it must have been difficult to see me with Mike."

Lisa shook her head. "I just don't understand. How can you be with someone else? I thought you loved Uncle Frank so much. He's only been gone . . ." Lisa covered her face with her hands. She had loved Uncle Frank so much, and the reality of his not being there with Aunt Jane was suddenly more than she could bear. She took a deep breath, then looked up at her aunt. "You loved Uncle Frank, didn't you, Aunt Jane?"

Aunt Jane walked over to the rocking chair and crouched next to her. Looking directly in her eyes, she placed a hand on Lisa's shoulder. "Of course I did, Lisa. I still do."

Lisa's eyes filled with hot tears.

"Honey, you know I loved your uncle more than life itself. I always will." Aunt Jane rose, then took a seat across from her on the bed before continuing. "For months after the funeral, I felt life was over for me. I felt I had no future without Frank; it was unbearable. Then, one Sunday morning, my pastor gave a message that reminded me of something I had long forgotten. My happiness and fulfillment in life cannot depend on those I love, no matter how much I love them. It can only be fulfilled through obedience to God and living my life fully in His love."

"Lisa, it's God's love that fulfills me now. Once I accepted that fact, I was able to begin to move on with life and open myself up to being happy again. Even to love again. First, to love myself and my life—that's how I began to heal. Frank is safe with his heavenly Father. I fully understand that now." Aunt Jane reached out and touched Lisa's face, gently wiping the tears from her cheek. "And God's plan for me is that I go on with my life."

"God's plan? The same God that let Ryan and Uncle Frank die?"

With those words, the floodgates of her wounded spirit opened wide, and she wept uncontrollably. There was no escaping the overwhelming grief and sorrow that consumed her, making it hard even to breathe.

"Oh, honey." Aunt Jane stood and pulled Lisa out of the chair, and in one quick motion, pulled her close into her arms. She squeezed her niece tightly and held her there while Lisa cried. But it wasn't Uncle Frank that Lisa cried for—not only for him, at least. It was for everything. For all the loss and pain and fear since her brother's diagnosis. So much had happened since that day. So much. And so much had been lost. Her faith in life—in any promises it held—it had all disappeared in a moment, and it was never coming back. She would never again feel the safety and peace that she'd felt before. Yes, it was her own faith in life that she mourned . . . that, and everything else.

After a while, Aunt Jane released her. "Enough tears now," she said, wiping Lisa's face with a tissue she drew from her skirt pocket.

Lisa took a long and shaky breath, then exhaled.

"There. That's better." Aunt Jane smiled. "Now. You must be hungry after your long road trip. And I think we need to get your things from the truck," she added with a wink, then held another tissue out to her.

Lisa took the tissue, and as Aunt Jane walked toward the door, she wiped the remaining tears from her face. "Hey, Aunt Jane?"

Aunt Jane stopped in the doorway and turned to face her. "Yes, honey?"

"I'm so sorry."

CHAPTER 6

Lisa's parents stood on the doorstep of Aunt Jane's farm. They had driven all night, they said, and they were exhausted. But something was different—they were smiling, and they were . . . happy!

She couldn't believe it!

The next few moments passed in a blur as they ushered her into their arms for a hug. Apologies and promises of a better future were made. The three of them were going to be a happy family again.

Suddenly, a loud crack of thunder startled Lisa awake. Her eyes snapped open. It had all been a dream.

"Darn it!"

Turning onto her side, Lisa glared at the clock on the nightstand. It was nearly midnight. Outside, dark clouds loomed overhead, and another clash of thunder sounded in the distance. A stiff breeze whipped the limbs of the tree outside against the glass windowpane. A storm was brewing.

Sleep so far had been restless. Just hours ago, she'd arrived at her aunt's farmhouse seeking relief from the troubles and pressures at home. Instead of finding relief, she now faced new challenges she had not expected. Two choices stood before her: She could go back home and try to accept things as they were, or she could stay to work things through with her aunt.

Lisa loved her aunt, and she had been there for her in good times and bad times. She needed that now. Really needed it. And it wasn't as if she had to like that Aunt Jane had a new boyfriend . . . But she could handle it. She could try to make the best out of an awkward situation.

Plus, it *was* her summer vacation.

Another thunderclap boomed above. There was no way she would go back to sleep with the way the storm was brewing outside. Peeling back the quilt, she slipped out of bed, put on her fluffy pink bathrobe and slippers, and headed downstairs.

Aunt Jane sat at the kitchen table, smiling. "I figured you'd be down eventually. I couldn't sleep myself." On the table before her were two slices of homemade apple pie and a tall glass of milk.

"Care to join me for a late-night snack? I realize we didn't get a chance to talk."

"Thanks," Lisa said, sliding onto the chair across from her aunt.

"Lisa, I'm sorry about today. I should have told you about Mike sooner. Honestly, I didn't expect him to be here when you arrived."

"Well, you could have . . . I wish . . . I wish someone had at least warned me."

"I know. I see that now." Aunt Jane pushed one of the plates of pie toward Lisa. "Now, how about some pie?"

Over the next hour, and after several slices of homemade apple pie, the two talked about school, the family, Uncle Frank, and Ryan. Just like Lisa knew she would, Aunt Jane spent most of the time simply listening as she opened her heart and shared her struggles and hurt.

For Lisa, just admitting she had problems was an incredibly good place to start.

The next morning, Lisa woke to the sun shining brightly through her bedroom window and the scent of coffee brewing in the kitchen. Aunt Jane was up already. Perfect. She really needed a hot cup of coffee. Slipping on her robe, she wiped the sleep from her eyes and headed downstairs.

Aunt Jane was sitting at the table with a hot cup of coffee and her Bible open in front of her.

"Good morning, honey. What would you like for breakfast?" She smiled. "How about my famous blueberry pancakes? I have fresh blueberries I just picked at Makowski's down the road."

"That sounds great. But no rush. I think I'll start with a hot cup of coffee." Lisa yawned, picked out a yellow mug with a big sunflower on it from the hooks underneath the cabinet, and poured herself a cup. She then held it up so she could read the inscription. She chuckled. *"Expect the Unexpected. Well, that's about right."*

Aunt Jane laughed too. "I'm glad to see your sense of humor has returned, honey."

After breakfast, Lisa called Scott. They decided to meet the following morning at his family's new place. She was excited to see him again, but she couldn't get past the feeling that something had changed between them. Once again, he'd seemed so distant. Maybe she was kidding herself. Too much time had passed; too many things had changed. Maybe their friendship could never be what it once was.

Scott sat in his room, deep in prayer. In just one day, Lisa would know the truth. This would either bring them closer as friends or drive a wedge between them. Either way, he had to be prepared.

Ever since the first call from Lisa, he'd felt a deep prompting to share with her not only his new circumstances but how they had changed him and his life. He needed to share with her his new relationship with Christ.

"Why me, Lord?" he prayed earnestly. "I don't think I'm ready for this."

Do not lose heart. Remember, I do not call the equipped; I equip the called. Trust in me.

Scott had heard before that sharing one's faith was something done not in our own strength or wisdom, but in God's. Until now, he hadn't understood what that really meant. His journey of faith had come full circle—the messages he'd heard as a child were now coming to life with all the power and understanding he had never known. Now it was his time to share that with someone else. He might not feel ready, but God had promised to equip him, and that was all he needed. God would get through to Lisa; he was just the messenger.

I think I get it now, Lord.

The fact was that Lisa was on a path destined for trouble. The signs were there even before Ryan died, and now he had the chance to make a difference in her life, to share his experience, and to help set her on the right path. Beneath Lisa's "tough cookie" exterior, there was a bit of himself—a scared kid looking for purpose and self-worth. It had become obvious that Lisa struggled to accept that she couldn't fix things on her own. In order to move on, she would first need to accept that. Only then would she be able to find and receive wholeheartedly the one who could change everything . . . God.

Scott, too, had tried to do it his own way. He'd been a stubborn, arrogant teenager, living life for his own excitement and self-gratification. He found all he thought he needed in sports, friends, and popularity. And then, he'd lost it all in one disastrous night. He didn't want anything like that to happen to Lisa.

I just hope I can reach her in time—before it's too late.

Wednesday morning, Lisa woke just as the sun was rising. She was beginning to feel more relaxed, and the rest had improved her attitude. Especially now that the shock of Aunt Jane's new boyfriend had worn off. Today, she would put the issue of Mike aside and enjoy the day.

Just as long as there were no more surprises.

She stretched, then shifted to the edge of the bed and got up. Sorting through her suitcase, she carefully picked out her clothes for the day and headed to the bathroom for a long, hot shower. Next on the agenda: catching up with Scott.

Scott. Just the thought of him brought a smile to her face. She couldn't help it! After two years without seeing him, she hoped they could rekindle their friendship. Hopefully the distance she sensed between them was only because they hadn't talked in a while. That must have been it. Once they saw each other, they'd be able to pick up right where they left off.

Maybe more. Maybe she'd even have a boyfriend by the end of summer. Stranger things had happened, right? Surely someday, someone was going to see her for the beauty she was.

Wow. She had always felt this place was special. Now, she truly believed it. Because for the first time since Ryan's death, she actually found herself feeling happy and hopeful about the future. Where usually she heard nothing but negative voices following her everywhere, reminding her she wasn't good enough or pretty enough, this self-assurance was something new.

I guess this summer vacation was a good idea after all.

"Someone's up early this morning," Aunt Jane said as Lisa bounded into the kitchen.

She'd chosen slim-cut dark blue jeans with a soft-blue, V-neck cashmere sweater, a pair of blue Converse sneakers, and aquamarine studded earrings for her visit with Scott. Hopefully Aunt Jane wouldn't give her a hard time about the extra effort she'd put into her look.

"I know. I couldn't sleep," Lisa said in a cheery tone. "I'm excited about seeing Scott today."

"You know, I'm really glad you're going to see him. I've often wondered what happened with their family. They moved away so quickly, and we haven't been in touch since. I guess we just lost touch after your Uncle Frank . . ." Aunt Jane stopped and seemed to become lost in thought for several seconds before suddenly returning to her task, cracking an egg into the bowl in front of her. "They did send me a nice sympathy card when he passed, though. I'm sorry we lost touch. We used to be so close." She cracked another egg into the bowl and then whipped them together with a metal whisk. "It will be nice for you to catch up with your old friend again. Maybe I'll finally have a chance to reconnect with his parents as well."

"I was thinking the same thing last night. Maybe we can change that this summer."

"I think you're probably right, Lisa. Every day is filled with new possibilities." Aunt Jane smiled. "I like this new attitude of yours."

Lisa smiled. So Aunt Jane had noticed a change, too. It wasn't just in her head. She couldn't quite explain it, but being at Aunt Jane's seemed to have sparked something deep within her. Was it a sense of freedom? The hope of a fresh start? She wasn't sure, but she was enjoying her newfound confidence for the future. Whatever it was, she wasn't going to take the summer and its opportunities for granted. This was going to be her time. Anything was possible, and she was hopeful and eager to see what would happen next.

"So, would you like some breakfast before you go?" Aunt Jane asked.

"No, thank you. I think I'm going to go ahead and head to the McCarthy's."

"Well, tell them I said hello, will you?"

"Sure thing," Lisa said, as she made her way out the squeaking kitchen screen door. "Bye, Aunt Jane."

Outside, Lisa took in the full view of the landscape. The sun beamed brightly against the pale blue sky, apple trees lined the property as far as the eye could see, and the air smelled of lilacs and honeysuckle. Everywhere she looked was another memory of summers past. She took a long, deep breath. If there had ever been heaven on earth, this would have been it.

This place certainly brings back memories.

Looking out toward the back of the property, she could barely make out the McCarthys' old house through the apple orchard. It was in the orchard that she and Scott had first played hide-and-seek. And there were the animal pens, where they had watched the baby goats play. So many things around her felt so familiar, and yet, so much had changed. It felt like a lifetime ago that she'd had to grow up and discover that childhood passes away too quickly. Its innocence was behind her now. Life wasn't as simple as it once was, and she wasn't the same girl Scott probably remembered.

Lisa hopped into Bluebell and started up the engine. She tapped on her phone's GPS and entered Scott's address. In only twenty minutes, they would finally be face to face.

She glanced up in the rear-view mirror and gave herself one last look. Scott would be surprised, all right. She sure wasn't the same awkward teenager tomboy she'd been the last time he'd seen her.

CHAPTER 7

Lisa stood at the McCarthy door, equally excited and nervous. She felt like a woman on the brink of the rest of her life. For the first time in years, she was ready for whatever could come her way.

Look out world! Here I come.

She reached forward confidently and gave the front door three solid knocks.

Slowly, the door opened.

In a single moment, Lisa's heart seemed to expand forcefully against her chest and her head filled with a loud pressure. This couldn't be real. This couldn't be Scott. And yet, there he was, smiling awkwardly up at her and sitting in a steel, gray wheelchair.

For a moment, she couldn't speak. It was as if time had stopped, and her voice had become lost somewhere between her mind and her gaping mouth. Now it all made sense: his family's selling the farm and moving into town, his awkwardness on the phone, his disappearance from her life just when she'd needed him the most. Not to mention the ramp she'd just walked up to reach the front door. How had she not realized?

"Scott?" she finally said. "What—?"

"Oh, please. It's not as bad as it looks. Now get in here and give me a hug."

Scott backed up his wheelchair. He waited as she stepped inside, then swung the door shut behind her. She leaned forward and hugged him awkwardly before quickly straightening, then he turned a hundred and eighty degrees and wheeled toward the living room. "Follow me."

Lisa followed him as he turned inside the doorway to the living room and wheeled his chair toward the couch. "I'm serious, Scott. What happened? And why didn't you tell me? You should have . . . you should have called, Scott!" Lisa's face grew suddenly hot.

He stopped and turned his chair to face her. "I know. I should have called you. It's just taken me a while to adjust to . . ." he held his hands out and shrugged, " . . . this."

"Yeah, but—"

"Look, I'm sorry. I know. But I wasn't sure how to tell you. Your family was already going through so much, and then your uncle died, so I just thought I'd wait, and . . . your life was already so complicated, you know."

"Not too complicated for this." The pounding in her head had subsided. She plopped down on one of the chairs across from the sofa. "Not too complicated for you." She looked him in the eyes and urged a smile to her lips.

They said nothing for several seconds, but their eyes stayed locked to each other's. Suddenly Scott turned his chair to the side and began wheeling away. "Would you like something to drink?" he asked over his shoulder. "I have a feeling what's coming next will take a while."

"Sure."

Scott maneuvered his way through the open living area and into the kitchen that ran across the back wall of the house. Lisa inhaled deeply and took in her surroundings for the first time since she'd arrived. She recognized some of the furnishings from the McCarthys' old farmhouse, but a lot was missing. As Scott opened the refrigerator and fished out a couple of sodas, it dawned on her that they would have needed to create space for his chair to move freely throughout the house.

Scott closed the refrigerator and made his way back to the living area with the two cans propped between his knees. He looked small and strangely vulnerable in his wheelchair. So different than how she remembered him. Although his arms were more muscular and his shoulders broader than before. Maybe from wheeling himself around in the chair all the time.

"I hope you don't mind; this is the best I could do. I still haven't gotten the hang of carrying glasses." He handed her the can, and she noticed a scar etched along the right side of his face.

Lisa took the can and popped off the lid. She quickly took a few sips, hoping he would break the silence. Her mind raced, but she couldn't think of a thing to say. She didn't know how to put into words what she was feeling. Was it him she felt bad for, or herself? Was she angry because he hadn't told her? That's what true friends were supposed to do, right? Tell each other their problems? But what if it was her fault? What if she'd been so caught up in her own problems that he felt like he couldn't tell her. Like she wouldn't have been there for him? The thought made her sick to her stomach.

Scott stopped fidgeting with the tab on his can and looked up at her. "You're mighty quiet over there. You okay?"

"I'm okay. It's just caught me off guard, that's all." Lisa said, pushing her thoughts aside for the moment.

"I know, right? Imagine my surprise." Scott chuckled, and a twinkle lit his eyes.

And there it was—that same confidence and sense of humor she'd always admired. Nothing ever seemed to fluster him. No matter what, he was always able to lighten any awkward situation with humor.

"So," she said, taking in another deep breath, "Tell me. What happened?"

Scott cracked the lid on his can and took a long drink. "Well," he said, wiping his mouth with the back of his hand, "I had a car accident, and I broke my back."

"When? When did all this happen? What do the doctors say? Will you be able to walk again? Tell me everything. I can't believe you didn't tell me, Scott!"

"Whoa, whoa," Scott held his hand a hand up and laughed. "Okay, okay. One question at a time. It's a long story, but we've got plenty of time to catch up."

He smiled, and Lisa felt her heart beating deeply in her chest.

"My injuries are pretty serious," he said, "and the doctors don't know if my situation will ever change. It's most likely permanent. Where I go from here pretty much depends on me."

"Well, if that's true, you'll be up and around in no time."

"I wish I had your confidence. It's been really tough, and I'd hoped to see more improvement by now." He looked at her for a moment, then something changed in his eyes. "So much has changed since we last saw each other; to be honest, I'm not so sure about much anymore."

Lisa was surprised by Scott's vulnerability. There was a softer, more serious side coming through. A side she'd never seen in him before.

"Okay, so what *exactly* happened? And how long has it been?"

"Oh, you know me, just our having a good time. The guys and I were hanging out, enjoying our summer of freedom, talking about college. We were playing basketball on the outside school court. It was after midnight by the time I headed home. I was exhausted, and something ran across the road, and, well, you can guess the rest." Scott shook his head. "Stupid, and look at what it cost me!"

Lisa was intrigued by his story; she couldn't quite explain it, but she felt there was more to it than he was telling.

"No, Scott, don't blame yourself! Things happen. Things out of our control."

"I understand that, but I made a choice, a dumb choice." His eyes shifted away. "It still hurts to think about it."

Scott took another long drink from the soda can. "So, what's been going on with you?"

His desire to change the subject was not lost on Lisa. Or the way he now seemed unable to look at her. There was more to the story, but she'd let it go for now. It couldn't be easy for him to relive everything. "Oh, you know." She leaned back in the seat. "This year has been really hard. I'm not doing so well in school. Actually, I totally screwed up. Let's just say you're not the only one with regrets." Lisa rolled her eyes. "And on top of that"—she took a long, steadying breath—"my parents have been talking about getting a divorce."

"Oh, Lisa! I'm so sorry." Scott wheeled closer and put a hand on her shoulder.

Lisa bit down hard on her lip to keep from crying. "Thanks. I'm just so tired of trying to make things work. I can't deal with it anymore."

"I bet. But Lisa, you can't change things between your parents. They have to do that for themselves."

"You're right, I know."

"Maybe being here this summer will be the best thing for all of you. You can take some time off, relax, and refocus on yourself and your life, and your parents have some time to work on things too."

She smiled. Hopefully, he was right.

Scott moved his hand from her shoulder. "You know," he said, again fidgeting with the soda can, "I'm really sorry I didn't check on you after your uncle died. I know it must have been tough, especially after losing Ryan."

"Yeah. Really hard."

"I really wish I'd been there for you."

"Thanks, Scott." She dabbed at her wet eyes, then threw her arms up. "Look at me. Here you are in a wheelchair, and I'm over here making it about me."

He smiled brightly, and the skin around his eyes crinkled. "Don't say that. From now on, I'll always be here for you, Lisa. I want you to know that."

The next few hours passed quickly as the two caught up on each other's lives. That was the beauty of true friendship; always being able to pick things up where they'd left off, as if there had never been any distance or time between them. Then again, things did feel a little different now; she'd felt it when he put his hand on her shoulder, and in the way they occasionally looked into each other's eyes. There was no denying their friendship remained intact, but the feelings she was experiencing today were beyond friendship, deeper and more intense.

I wonder if he feels the same way.

Looking again into his blue eyes, Lisa felt more like a woman than ever before. They weren't kids anymore; they were young adults with new emotions and passions. She was drawn intensely to this new version of Scott. He had faced the harsh reality of death and come out stronger for it. She couldn't quite explain it, but there seemed to be an inner strength she hadn't seen before. Where had it come from? She didn't know, but something told her she was going to find out. She had to.

"Scott Lucas McCarthy, you didn't tell me we had company!"

"Hey, Mom." Scott turned to where his mom stood smiling from the kitchen doorway, her arms full of groceries.

"Lisa and I have just been doing some catching up."

Lisa rose from the chair, and his mom set the bags on the kitchen table, scurried over to her, and wrapped her in an exuberant hug. As they held on to each other, Scott couldn't help but notice how much his friend had changed since he'd last seen her. She sure wasn't the little girl he'd first met all those years ago.

"We were so shocked to hear about Uncle Frank, dear." His mom released Lisa from her embrace but held her by the arms. "I just hate that we were out of town when it happened. How is your aunt? I hope she's doing okay."

Lisa flinched. "She is. "

"And your parents, how are they doing? It's all just so heartbreaking."

"Well . . ." Lisa glanced down at her watch. "Oh gosh, I should be going. Aunt Jane will be wondering where I am." She stepped back and shot Scott a "help me" smile.

"Mom," he said, taking Lisa's hints, "there will be plenty of time to catch up later. She's staying with her aunt most of the summer."

Mrs. McCarthy looked at them both. She opened her mouth as if to say something, but stopped. "All right then," she said. "But don't you dare be a stranger. I feel bad we haven't stayed in touch. We need to fix that."

"I won't." Lisa smiled warmly, then turned back to him. "Well, I should be going."

Scott led Lisa out of the room and to the front of the house. He pulled the door open for her.

Lisa stopped on her way out and turned back to him. "I'll catch you guys later, I promise!"

"You do that," he said, and then winked before closing the door behind her and returning to the living room.

"Was it something I said?" His mother looked confused.

"No, it's not that. Lisa's just been through a lot this year."

"Well, we certainly understand that, don't we? I hope everything turns out all right for her; let her know we're around if she ever needs anything, okay?"

"I will. Thanks, Mom."

As she made her way back to the kitchen and began putting the groceries away, Scott whispered a prayer of relief. He was glad his mother hadn't inquired further; otherwise, he'd have been compelled to tell her everything about the Sanchez family troubles. Now, he didn't have to make a choice.

Scott wheeled to his bedroom and closed the door behind him. He completely respected the Sanchez family's need for privacy. Yes, this was their story to tell, and it would remain that way as long as he and Lisa were friends. Hadn't she just done the same for him, not pressuring him for more details about his accident?

On the other hand, he could see the effect her situation was having on her, and it just wasn't right. In the couple of hours they'd spent together, she'd been able to share so much of what she'd been facing lately, and her parents' relationship was just one part of it. The deaths of her brother and uncle, her subsequent struggles at school and the strained family dynamics were more than enough to deal with, and then she'd come here to have to cope with the idea of her Aunt Jane's new boyfriend, Mike. What more did God have planned for her?

Son, I know the road ahead. Remember the promise I set forth for you in Jeremiah 29:11: "For I know the plans I have for you. To give you a future and a hope."

He needed to remind himself that this promise applied to everyone, including Lisa. But, most importantly, he needed to remember that God had a plan, and it wasn't his job to figure things out.

I know. But I don't know how much more of this Lisa can take. Her family has been through enough as it is. Their future is in question. How is Lisa supposed to understand a loving God when her world is falling apart? And I'm supposed to be the one to tell her how to change her life.

He had changed his life, and he was grateful for his second chance, but he had also made many mistakes along the way. He didn't want to make any mistakes with Lisa. He needed to be more confident that he had changed enough to make the right choices.

Talking to Lisa had rekindled so many memories from the past. They had gone from two carefree kids chasing his dog, Brutus, through the field, to close teenaged friends at the local Dover Road Dari Ice Cream Shop eating double scoop ice cream cones and talking about their lives at home, Ryan's illness, and their dreams for the future. Scott used to dream of playing basketball professionally. He was the star player on the basketball team and was featured on the cover of the local paper numerous times as he led the team to state championships. Lisa dreamed of being a writer or a poet, and she would often share with him some of her favorite books and even the poems she had written.

But he wasn't that same guy anymore. All his dreams had been crushed in an instant. He was a cripple now. A *cripple*. So what now? What could he offer anyone? How was he supposed to make something of himself in this wheelchair? With college scholarships no longer an option, he was at an impasse.

Scott stared at his bedroom wall lined with shelves filled with trophies, pictures of his high school achievements, and mementos of his past. On one shelf was a trophy from Little League when he was only ten. "Most Valuable Player," the little brass plate read. Newspaper clippings lay strewn next to it from articles on his winning games and a picture of him surrounded by all his teammates, holding the trophy from the State Basketball Championship. He found it hard to look at them these days.

Why had God spared his life only to confine him to a wheelchair? Was this all just punishment for his bad behavior?

Now, in the midst of everything—the uncertainty about his future and Lisa's arrival—he was just beginning to understand the meaning of walking by faith. His parents had done their best to instill a firm foundation of faith and Christian values, but believing in them wasn't enough. He had to act on them as well.

Scott's gaze turned upward. Before he could help Lisa, he had a lot of thinking to do. And a lot of praying, too.

CHAPTER 8

"I'm back!" Lisa let the kitchen screen door slam behind her, anxious to find Aunt Jane. "You won't believe what's happened to Scott."

No answer.

Come to think of it, Aunt Jane's car hadn't been outside when she pulled up. She'd been so excited to talk to her about everything that happened at Scott's and try to make sense of all the feelings and thoughts swirling in her mind that she hadn't even noticed it was missing.

"That's odd," she said to herself. Aunt Jane hadn't said she was going anywhere this afternoon. She must have gone out to run some errands. Sure enough, on the entry table, a note awaited her. It read: *Hope you enjoyed catching up with Scott. You'll have to fill me in. I ran out to get a few groceries. Be back later! FYI: I've invited Mike to join us for dinner tonight. Please keep an open mind. See you soon. Jane*

Lisa traced the corners of the note with her fingertips. Over the last 2 days, she'd had thought a lot about her initial reaction to Mike. Maybe she'd been wrong to judge him so quickly. She had heard before, "You can't help whom you fall in love with." Didn't Aunt Jane deserve that opportunity? She did, and Lisa was determined to give him a fair chance. Starting tonight.

What an exhausting vacation this had quickly become. First, she found her aunt kissing a stranger, and now she finds out her good friend Scott may be permanently in a wheelchair. What was next? She didn't know, but one thing had become abundantly clear, she would have to decide what she wanted for herself, regardless of life's circumstances. If that meant developing a backbone and making her own choices for a change, so be it. Starting with college. She wasn't sure if college was the right choice for her. It should be her decision about what she does after high school. Whatever she decided, her parents would just have to accept that.

She grabbed her backpack and threw it on the bed. Rummaging through the side pocket, she pulled out a small notebook and a pen and began a list. At the top of the page, she wrote: *Choices for My Future.*

Hours after her visit, Scott still couldn't get Lisa off his mind. As much as he wanted to share his faith with her, the visit had stirred emotions in him he hadn't expected. He couldn't deny his feelings were more than just those for a friend. He was attracted to this new version of Lisa. But she had been through a lot in the past two years; the last thing he wanted was to make things more complicated than they were already. The next step was obvious—telling her about his faith.

Does she realize it yet, Lord? That she needs You. Is her heart tired of living day by day and trying to please everyone around her? Everyone, that is, except You. Because in the end, You're the only one that really matters.

She recognizes the need, Scott! The door is open; all she needs to do is walk through it. You can show her the way.

But how, Lord?

Don't worry about that, son. The opportunity is approaching. Just be prepared.

Scott accepted the challenge with a bit of apprehension.

There was a light knocking at his bedroom door.

"Scott," his mom said. "Is everything all right?"

"Yes, Mom. I'm fine." He glanced at the clock. It was almost six o'clock and time for his father to return home from work.

Scott's mom opened the door and slipped into the room.

"You've been spending a lot of time in your room lately. Are you okay? I don't want you to start slipping back into old patterns."

He held up his hand. "I'm fine, Mom." He smiled. "Don't start worrying. I've just been contemplating my life. What's happened to me, and where I want to go from here. It's time I started planning for my future. It doesn't look like I'll be getting out of this chair any time soon. Maybe never."

"Well, I'm glad you are starting to think about your future, son." She leaned against the doorframe. "Your dad should be home anytime now, and I'm sure he'd like to hear all about it at dinner."

"Yeah. Maybe so."

"Well, I'll leave you alone. Let me know if you need me." She shut the door behind her, and as her footsteps faded, Scott returned to his thoughts.

God, I am truly blessed to be part of this family. I know not everyone is as lucky as I am.

His parents had done so much for him since the accident. Still, he couldn't get over how overprotective they had become. Before the accident, they trusted him—probably more than they should have—and gave him a lot of freedom. Now, it seemed they had a constant eye on him.

He hadn't noticed the change until a few weeks after coming home from the hospital. At first everyone was just so grateful to have him home; it didn't matter what they had to do as a family to help him. His mother adapted her busy schedule to get Scott out of bed, get him dressed and tend to his personal needs, and take him to physical therapy three times a week. She never complained—no one in the family did. Not even when they had to make the difficult decision to sell the farm they loved and make them move into a one-story home in town so Scott could have a first-floor bedroom. They had done everything they could to make his life more comfortable.

In the beginning, Scott welcomed all the help and attention. Even his younger brothers tried to be helpful, taking over his chores, mowing the lawn, taking the trash out, feeding their dog, Brutus, whatever they could do to help. There was more family time as well. Friday became game night, and his parents made a point of the family spending time with him every day.

Scott was used to being the center of attention, but not in this way, and it wasn't long before the feeling of being so dependent on others for the simplest tasks left him feeling helpless. He began to struggle with depression. His dependence on his family, lack of physical activity, and loneliness took a toll on him. He missed his friends, he missed playing basketball and sometimes felt smothered by his parents.

It's crazy, Lord. It's almost like they live to help me, and if I attempt to do anything for myself, they expect me to break.

I know, my son! Continue to be strong in Me; in all things, I have a purpose.

Let's hope I'm as strong as you think I am.

Lisa dug out her Algebra book and slammed it on the kitchen table. "Ugh!"

Well, she had to start sometime. Might as well be today.

She'd worked for nearly an hour before she heard her aunt's car crunching up the driveway.

"Finally, she's back." She slammed the book closed and shoved it across the table. She could finally stop studying.

Within seconds, Aunt Jane was pushing the screen door open with her hip. "So, how did your visit with Scott go today?" She dropped two paper bags of groceries on the counter and began emptying them.

"Pretty well, considering what they've gone through."

"Did you know Scott was in an accident? He's paralyzed now and in a wheelchair. They don't know if he'll ever walk again!"

Aunt Jane gasped and stopped unloading the groceries. "What? Are you serious?" She walked over to where Lisa sat. "I'd heard Scott had an accident, but with your Uncle Frank dying I guess I was just in my own little world. But I'm so sorry to hear that."

"I know. It's . . . it's . . . I don't even know what to think, honestly."

"So . . ." She pulled out a chair and sat next to Lisa. "How was he?"

"He seemed okay, I guess. All things considered. In some ways he was just the same old Scott."

"I'm sure he was happy to see you. You guys were always so close." She placed a hand on Lisa's. "And how are you? I'm sure this news must have hit you pretty hard."

"It's a lot, for sure. But I'll be okay. I guess."

"Well, you let me know if you need to talk about it. You know I'm here for you." Aunt Jane sat quietly for a moment, then stood and returned to emptying the groceries. "Why don't you get back to that book while I put the groceries away and start dinner. Mike will be here soon."

Lisa rolled her eyes. " Ugh!" she said, opening the book. "More algebra."

"So, Mike, tell me again what you do." Lisa forked at her food as the three of them sat at the kitchen table having dinner.

"Well, by day, I'm a handyman down at Cedar Hills Apartments, just down the road from the church. But I spend my spare time at the church helping with repairs and building projects. That's how I met your aunt." Mike smiled adoringly at Aunt Jane.

"I remember," Aunt Jane said. "I couldn't get over how straightforward you were. You almost scared me away."

"But then, you got to know me and realized I wasn't such a bad guy. That's something I hope you'll recognize someday, too, Lisa."

He smiled again, this time at Lisa, and there was something oddly familiar and soothing about it. Yes, in some strange way, Mike reminded her of her uncle.

Dinner was relaxed, and the conversation casual, for which Lisa was grateful. It had already been a full day, and she had no interest in getting into anything serious. After a delicious dinner of steak, parsley potatoes, and homemade bread, Mike helped Jane clear the table and pile the dishes in the sink. Lisa watched the ease with which they worked together, as well as the small moments of intimacy. A slight touch of the hand when Aunt Jane passed a dish along to Mike or the smile that crossed her face when she caught him looking at her.

She was really beginning to see the joy Mike brought to her aunt's life.

Deciding to give them privacy, Lisa excused herself, but as she headed toward the stairs, Mike spoke up.

"I've been waiting all week for this, Jane. I know it might not be the best timing, but . . . He suddenly dropped to one knee in front of Aunt Jane.

"Mike, what are you doing?"

"I don't want to wait a minute longer. We aren't getting any younger, and since your niece is here for the summer . . ."

"It's too soon. Isn't it?"

"I know it seems sudden, Jane, but I just can't go another day without telling you how I feel. I want to spend the rest of my life with you."

The rest of the conversation faded as Lisa stood at the bottom of the stairs, mouth wide open.

This couldn't be happening. Aunt Jane was right; it was too soon. Marriage? Dating, maybe, but *marriage*! No! Aunt Jane had barely gotten over the loss of Uncle Frank. And now what? She was getting a replacement.

She had heard enough. She didn't care what Mike thought of her anymore; she was through playing nice. Someone had to be the voice of reason and tell it like it was.

Before she realized what she was doing, she heard herself speaking.

"I honestly don't believe you, Mike!" She stormed back into the kitchen. "If you claim to love so much, why can't you wait? You've only been dating for . . . I don't know what? Like a minute?"

"Lisa, honey." Aunt Jane reached for her, but she pulled away.

"You know what? No matter how hard you try, you can never replace Uncle Frank! So just forget it!"

With that, she stomped out of the kitchen and up the stairs.

"Lisa, may I come in?" Mike's voice made its way through the locked guestroom door.

"No. Please, just go away. I don't want to talk to you."

"No, Lisa, I'm not leaving until we talk."

Lisa waited for what felt like several minutes, listening for the sound of footsteps retreating. She heard nothing. She had begun to think he'd managed to slip away silently, when there was a gentle knock at the door.

"Lisa, please."

Great. Apparently if she wanted to get rid of him, she would have to suck it up and get it over with. Lisa stood and walked slowly to the door. "Excuse the mess," she said as she swung the door open, suddenly embarrassed by the room. She cleared a pile of clothes from her bed and plopped back down onto it. "Just say what you want to say, and then, please leave me alone."

"Lisa . . ." Mike started slowly, easing himself only a small step into the room.

"Yes?"

"Lisa, listen. I know this is difficult for you, and I completely understand your concern."

"You can't possibly understand."

"Believe it or not, I do. And I know you don't know me at all. But I was in your shoes once."

"Oh, really?"

The sarcasm felt satisfying as it rolled off her tongue, like a release valve for her anger. But when Mike returned only a gentle smile, there was a twinge of guilt she couldn't deny.

"When I was just a little younger than you, my father died. It was quite unexpected. Overnight, my mom became my entire world. All we had was each other. Eventually, though, she started dating. I was furious. Not only did I feel my mom was betraying my father, but I felt like she was betraying me as well. Like she was choosing someone else over us and our special bond." He closed his eyes and took a deep breath before continuing. "I started acting out, skipping school, hanging out with the wrong crowd. My mom thought it would be good for us to have family therapy, and to be honest, it helped me a lot."

"So, what? You're saying I need therapy?"

Mike chuckled, "No. That's not what I'm saying. But I sure did. I'm just saying it took a while for me to accept the situation. I wanted my mom to be happy, but it was still difficult for me."

"So . . . what happened?"

"I eventually opened up to the possibilities, and one day my mom found a really great guy. A guy I now call 'Dad.'

"Look, Lisa, what I'm trying to say is, I hope you'll give me a chance. I love your aunt. I will never hurt her, and I will give her all the time she needs to decide what's right for her. We understand your feelings, but you don't need to be angry or fearful."

"As for your uncle, I'm not trying to replace him. I only want to be a part of this family, a part of your aunt's life. And I hope we can be friends as well."

Lisa didn't respond. She really didn't know what to say. Part of her wanted to let go—she couldn't think of any reason to dislike Mike. But another part of her wanted to let the anger take over. To stop fighting and just let it win. To wrap herself up in it and let it insulate her from the world.

"Do you have anything you want to ask me?"

She shook her head.

"Well, that's all I wanted to say. I'll leave you alone now, but I'll be around if you want to talk."

Once Mike left, Lisa sat in her room, feeling both proud of herself and a bit self-conscious. She wasn't used to being so forward or blunt, but she had said what she thought, and that was that. After a few minutes her aunt's voice made its way from outside and through her window. She rose and peered out long enough to see Mike and her aunt embracing by the car.

I bet she said yes. I bet she told him she'd marry him.

"Unbelievable!"

No, the evening certainly hadn't gone as she'd hoped. She'd tried; she'd really tried to have an open mind and give Mike a second chance. But his little move had made it impossible. Asking her aunt to marry him?

What was he thinking? It was too soon. And while she'd taken a risk expressing her feelings, she was only trying to stand up for Aunt Jane. But, as usual, they'd dismissed her concerns for another emotional childish tantrum. Just like at home—she'd been treated like a child.

And, yes, Mike had tried to assure her he only had good intentions toward her aunt, but Lisa didn't know or trust him. At least not yet. She could admit she'd connected with his story about his father, but, really, that had nothing to do with her aunt or what was going on now. Although, as much as she hated to admit it, Aunt Jane did seem happy. But was that really what Uncle Frank would have wanted? For her to be happy with another man?

Oh, Uncle Frank, if only you were here to help me make sense of this. I'm just so confused.

With that, she crumbled onto the bed and cried herself to sleep.

CHAPTER 9

"Let's finish this game, boys, and then it's off to bed." Mr. McCarthy eyed the two young boys as he placed a card on top of the discard pile on the table. "It's been a long day for everyone, including you two."

"But Dad . . ." the boys whined in unison.

"No buts," Mrs. McCarthy said, turning from the kitchen sink to give the younger of her three boys her "I'm serious" look. "You heard your father. Finish your game and then off to bed."

"Okay, Mom." The boys chuckled at each other as they refocused on the game. It wasn't long before Owen called out "Uno" and raised his hands in triumph.

"I want a rematch," his brother shouted, pushing his brother.

"Oh no you don't. Not tonight anyway." Mr. McCarthy said, corralling the two brothers as they began pushing and shoving their way through the kitchen door and down the hall.

"Make sure they brush their teeth, Owen." Mrs. McCarthy said to her husband as he, too, disappeared from view.

Scott sat at the table smiling. It was nights like this that made him genuinely appreciate his life. He had a wonderful family that loved and enjoyed each other. Not once since the accident had his parents made him feel like a burden. And, despite the changes in his relationships with friends, his family never gave him much time to feel neglected. They made sure that he never spent too much time alone and had pulled him out of more than one spiral toward depression.

At first, after the accident, Scott was surrounded by both family and friends. He woke up in the hospital room with flowers and cards all around him. And in the weeks following, too, dozens of concerned friends visited him, encouraging him, reading to him, and sharing stories from school. As time went on, however, the number of visitors grew smaller as people returned to their routines. Scott's family, however, continued to visit daily, and his younger brothers sat on his bed, sharing sports magazines or comics with him.

By the end of his hospital stay, his friends rarely visited. That is, except for Gary, a guy from school he barely knew. He didn't run in the same crowds as Scott, but he had been in some of his classes, and they had always been cordial with each other. Gary continued in his regular visits all the way to the end.

His perspective began to change when Gary invited him to the youth group at his church. He assured Scott not only that the building was accessible, but also that he would love the group of kids who attended and have a blast. After multiple invitations, Scott finally gave in and went.

Gary was right—he had a blast.

Maybe it was because the kids were all strangers, but Scott didn't feel the same expectations he had with his old friends. For the first time in months, he felt like he could just be himself. The feeling was such a relief. He finally felt he had a fresh start. A fresh start for the new Scott.

He still had plenty of days of self-pity—days that would later give him shame for the way that he treated his family, particularly his parents, who were giving so much to help him with the transition. But now, he was finding a new source of hope. He had learned that prayer and simply talking to God strengthened his resolve and provided the strength he needed to get through the tough days when he struggled with depression or anger. As he read the New International Bible Gary had given him, he started building a new life based on faith in Christ.

When Scott started sliding back into old habits, he often prayed aloud: *Forgive me, Lord, there's the old Scott again.* And when he treated his parents or his brothers unkindly: *Forgive me for being angry—again, Lord.*

Before long, his outbursts of temper had become less frequent and his battle against depression more manageable. Prayer was a part of Scott's daily routine as he leaned on God and trusted in His love and forgiveness.

Cindy, one of the girls Scott met in Gary's youth group, had given him a book by a woman named Joni Eareckson Tada, who, at seventeen, had been in a diving accident that had left her paralyzed from the neck down. Scott related to her story, as she described herself as being "trapped." Trapped in a body that would no longer respond to her direction. Despite her struggles, she found hope as she learned to trust in God and to rely on Him to teach her what it meant to live a full and vibrant life.

As he was approaching his nineteenth birthday, Scott began thinking about his future. He had been told that people in his condition typically live a normal lifespan, marry, and have productive lives. It all came down to their attitudes and ability to accept their condition and realize their potential. The question that faced him was, now that basketball and an athletic scholarship were no longer an option, what would he do with his life? Would he ever find a girl who could accept him the way he was? Would he ever find love and get married?

Then, his prayer often became, *Lord, help me. I need you. I worry about my future; help me trust in you.*

"The boys are asleep," Mr. McCarthy said, making his way back into the kitchen. "Now my vacation officially starts!"

That's right, Dad's job.

Amidst the excitement of the last few days, Scott had almost forgotten his dad's announcement that he'd been laid off. He had worked faithfully for almost twenty years for the MedElite Corporation as a spokesperson and well-respected pharmacist in his community, ensuring his customers received quality medications and around-the-clock consultations. Starting tomorrow, that would all change. The company was downsizing, laying off dozens of loyal employees while they reevaluated their options for possible relocation. His dad had done his best to mask the uncertainty of the situation by calling it a "vacation," but Scott knew his father better than that—he was concerned. He wouldn't consider moving away from the roots his family had planted in the community, but what other options were available locally was unclear.

The timing is perfect, Lord!

His father could use a distraction during this challenging time, and helping his oldest son navigate his changing relationship with Lisa might give him something else to focus on. Besides, Scott couldn't do it alone. He'd thought and prayed so much in the days after Lisa's visit about all she'd shared with him, yet so many questions and uncertainties remained.

It seemed to him that in all the chaos of Ryan's illness, Lisa had gotten lost. He could understand the time it took for her parents to care for Ryan during his illness—it was a full-time job for them—but the consequence of that was Lisa disappearing into the background.

Not once had she ever expressed any resentment toward Ryan for it—his needs always came first for her too. But even in her selflessness, she became lost. Her problems took second place. Not only for herself, but for her parents as well. It wasn't as if they didn't love her, but they didn't seem to have time for her, and this resulted in her feeling unloved. Scott had witnessed it the last summer they visited. Even then, her lively spirit had begun to fade.

He'd noticed it at the picnic the Mitchells hosted the summer they visited; Ryan was in remission. Scott had been drawn into the adults' conversation, as the excitement over his sports opportunities and potential sponsorships by several companies had become the topic of conversation. Lisa sat at the end of the table in a pair of cut-off blue jeans, her hair pulled up in a ponytail. She sat with her back toward the adults; she seemed absorbed in her own thoughts.

Scott was hoping to break away from the conversation and take a walk with her, but before he knew it, he was enjoying the attention and praise he was receiving from the adults far too much. Still, he noticed when Lisa got up and headed toward the house. He also noticed when she returned wearing a yellow sundress with her hair brushed out. Was it for his benefit? He wasn't sure, but he definitely noticed. And he was surprised by the flutter in his stomach when he saw her step down from the porch in that dress.

Mrs. McCarthy continued with the last of the dinner clean-up while Scott and his dad retired to the living room. Mr. McCarthy sat in his favorite recliner, picked up his Bible from the coffee table, and began his regular evening reading.

"Dad, can I ask you something personal?" Scott wheeled up in front of his dad's easy chair and leaned his elbows on the armrests of his chair.

Mr. McCarthy put down his Bible and looked at him. "Sure, Scott. What is it?"

"Well, Lisa's in town for the summer . . ." Scott began slowly, choosing his words carefully. "Her family has really been struggling since Ryan's death. I think she's at a crossroads and could use some answers. Real ones—that kind only God can offer. I want to share my faith with her without coming on too strong or jeopardizing our friendship. I care about her, Dad, and I can tell she's really hurting. How do I help her?"

Scott stopped himself from going too far. If he weren't careful, his father would figure things out, and then he might question his motives. Sure, he was developing deeper feelings for her, but that didn't mean things had to be complicated, right? In fact, it should make things a lot simpler; he genuinely cared about her and worried about her future.

Mr. McCarthy stood and walked the room as he spoke. "Son, witnessing to someone can be challenging; a delicate balance of compassion and honesty is needed. It takes courage. You should share your own personal experience, and then, based on Scripture, their need for a Savior.""

"Specifically for Lisa, just tell her how much God has changed your life. Be honest. Make sure she realizes the importance of the decision. That it's not something to be taken lightly. It must be a matter of personal faith. Her choice."

"Your father's right, sweetie." Mrs. McCarthy entered the room wiping her wet hands on a dishtowel. "She needs to find her own way in the process. You have to give her that freedom. Sometimes that can be the hardest part."

"You mean the freedom to find God on her own?"

"Exactly, son," his mother said. "Otherwise, she might come into a relationship with God with expectations that aren't biblical. For example, she might believe life will instantly change, and all her problems will disappear. You know God doesn't always take our problems away, but He will get us through them." Mrs. McCarthy's voice quivered slightly. "You know the truth of that as well as anyone."

"You mean my accident?" Scott didn't like to see his mother getting emotional, but this was important. If his accident and the lessons he and his family had learned could help reach Lisa, maybe some good could come from it.

His mom nodded. "People viewed your accident as a terrible tragedy; you had so much going for you, and in one night, it was all gone. But we believe 'all things work together for good' in God's plan for our lives. These new obstacles developed in you a solid foundation of moral character and a deep dependence on God that is essential for Christian living."

"I understand all of that," Scott said, "but, I have to admit, I still don't understand why God allows trials after Christians accept His gift of salvation and have turned their lives over to Him? If He is a loving Father, shouldn't we be able to expect good things from Him?"

"Life is a constant struggle, Scott," His father said. "But along with those struggles, we can't forget all the wonderful things God brings into our lives. We try to appreciate those and be grateful."

"That's right," his mother said. "Building a relationship with God doesn't happen overnight. That's what makes our foundation so strong. Only through these trials and spiritual growth can we build our faith, learn something about ourselves, and build a relationship with God through Jesus, our savior and our friend. We sure didn't expect the trials we've faced, and they have been hard to accept at times, but we know God has a plan."

"You know, people always say, 'seeing is believing,' but that's not what faith is about. If we knew what our future held and could physically see God, we wouldn't need our faith, and there would be no growth." His mother added. "We accept struggles as an opportunity to grow in faith. And we trust in a good God who knows what's best in the end."

"Thanks, guys. I appreciate your honesty. You've certainly given me a lot to consider and think about."

"You're welcome, Scott," his father said. "We're always here if you have more questions, and we are so proud of you for your concern for Lisa. We're always here if you need us. But remember, God is too."

Yes, that was one thing he knew for certain.

CHAPTER 10

"Rise and shine, lazy bones! You're not going to sleep all day. Not on my watch."

Aunt Jane's slender shadow crossed the room, peeling back the curtains and allowing morning sunrays to pour through the windows.

"Didn't your mother ever teach you to knock?" Lisa said, pulling the covers over her head.

"Ahh, but you forgot one important fact, my darling. This is my house. You've got twenty minutes to get dressed and meet me downstairs. We're going out for breakfast."

As Aunt Jane made her way downstairs, Lisa fumed inside. What nerve she had, completely dismissing last night and acting like it never happened. Aunt Jane had made her choice perfectly clear, hadn't she? Uncle Frank was a part of her past, Mike was her future, and she had no intention of turning the clock back now.

Either way, I can't turn down a free meal. Breakfast really did sound great.

Lisa hurried into the bathroom, washed her face, and brushed her teeth. She grabbed a clean pair of jeans, her favorite Minnie Mouse T-shirt, and quickly dressed.

Jane waited anxiously for Lisa at the bottom of the staircase. She'd spent much time the night before praying for a way to get through to her niece and hoped this breakfast would provide the fresh start they both needed. The last thing she wanted was to have her mad at her again.

Oh, Frank, if only you were here. He'd know how to get through to Lisa. How was she going to do this without him?

Consider it pure joy, my daughter, whenever you face trials of many kinds, because you know the testing of your faith builds perseverance.

This declaration from God's Word rose from the depths of her heart, strengthening and enveloping her. So much of the previous year she'd lived and breathed this verse from the book of James. Why should this trial be any different?

Because I never expected to witness to Lisa alone.

It had always been her and Frank's plan to do it together. But now, she'd have to do her best and leave the rest to God.

"You all right?" Lisa asked, stepping up behind her, her voice noticeably kinder than before.

"Yes." Jane grabbed her sunglasses and handed Lisa the car keys. "But why don't you go ahead and drive. My allergies are going haywire." She hated lying, but this was neither the time nor the place to start a deeper discussion. That would have to wait until she and Lisa reached their final destination.

Outside, Jane opened the passenger side and hopped in.

"Where to?" Lisa said.

"Just take a right onto Main Street; there's the Pancake Place on the right, just at the edge of town."

After sitting down in a corner booth and looking over the menu, Lisa ordered a plate of All-American favorites—a short stack of pancakes, eggs sunny side up, and a pile of golden hash browns. Jane took a healthy route, ordering a bowl of fruit alongside cottage cheese. The server brought a pot of hot coffee and poured a cup for Jane.

Lisa stared out the window.

"So how are things at home?" Jane said, breaking the silence. "I mean, really?"

Lisa slowly turned away from the window. "Honestly, things are falling apart back home. Mom and Dad are barely talking to each other." Lisa scoffed. "Not that we talked that much in the first place. And, as you know, I'm not doing well at school. Mom and Dad are always mad at me. Sometimes I just don't know what to do."

"I'm sorry I haven't been there for your family this past year. I had every intention of coming to visit, but after what happened, I was just so lost. Your family was having a hard enough time. I felt my grief would only make it harder for all of you."

"You could have at least called. My parents needed you. I needed you."

Jane felt her heart breaking into pieces with every word Lisa spoke. The truth hurt, and it was clear that by staying away, she had caused more injury to her family than she'd avoided.

"I know, sweetheart, and I'm so sorry for that. I did what I could at the time. I'm sure your mother understands. She knows what my grief felt like. But still, I will try to be there for all of you in the future." Jane reached out and covered her niece's hand with her own. "You know I love you, Lisa."

Lisa smiled.

"That was delicious," Lisa said as she smothered her last bit of pancake in syrup.

"Would you like a refill?" The waitress inquired.

"No thank you," Aunt Jane replied. "Just the check please."

Lisa watched in silence as her aunt paid the bill. She'd missed this, being able to talk to her aunt without fearing judgment or criticism. Still, she feared the invitation to breakfast had strings attached and that her aunt had an ulterior motive.

Back in the car, her suspicions were confirmed.

"I want to take you somewhere." Her aunt said, looking over at her from the passenger's seat.

Ah ha!

Lisa started the car. "Where exactly?"

"It's a surprise," Aunt Jane said mischievously, retrieving her sunglasses from her purse and putting them back on. "But it's somewhere very special to me."

Aunt Jane directed her to a road that led out of town, and they drove silently for several miles until they came up on a narrow dirt road overhung by dense bellowing willows.

"Turn right here. And hang on; things can get a little bumpy down here."

Within moments, the two were surrounded by nothing but trees. Lisa's eyes were captivated as streams of sunlight pierced through the forest's darkness, casting spotlights on the ground below.

"It's so beautiful. How did you find this place?" Lisa asked.

"It's a long story. It was weeks after your uncle died. I was tired of taking condolence calls and trying to put on a brave face for everyone. I just couldn't do it. So I decided to leave the house."

Aunt Jane was quiet for several seconds, and when Lisa glanced over at her, it seemed as if she were reliving the experience over again.

"I didn't know what to do, so I got in the car and just started driving. To nowhere, I guess. Then I saw this narrow little road, just off to my right, barely noticeable. It seemed to be going nowhere. Instinctively, I turned down it." Aunt Jane's smile was magic. "Then I found this place."

After Aunt Jane directed her to park the car on a flat, grassy spot at the side of the road, they climbed out of the car and headed down a narrow path leading into the woods. Lisa trailed behind.

"You coming or what?" Aunt Jane playfully called back to her.

She didn't need to be asked twice. She quickly caught up with her aunt and continued into the woods until they came to a small clearing. Canadian geese glided on a small pond surrounded by an assortment of vibrant wildflowers. The air was fresh with the scent of pines. Besides being breathtaking, the place exuded a sense of peace she had never experienced.

It was . . . complete solitude.

No wonder Aunt Jane loved it here. Just you and you alone with your thoughts. A perfect place to release every bit of pent-up emotion you have built up inside, and no one to hear you cry. Or, for that matter, scream.

Lisa chuckled softly.

"What?" Aunt Jane tilted her head.

"Oh, nothing. I was just thinking how this would be a wonderful place to . . . I don't know." Lisa shook her head.

"Scream?"

They both burst into laughter.

"Yeah, I thought so, too. And, believe me, I've taken advantage of the opportunity. The love of my life was gone, and he wasn't coming back. That's one of the harshest realities anyone will face, living without a loved one. You understand, don't you? Losing someone close to you can evoke a mixture of emotions, sorrow, as well as anger.

"This is where I come and talk to Frank. I cry and tell him how much I miss him. I read somewhere that there are seven stages to grief; each is a stepping-stone to the next. This place helped me through the process. If I hadn't found it . . . well, honestly, I don't think I would have survived. I was lost for a long time."

"What do you mean, lost?"

Aunt Jane looked past her to the trees beyond for a moment before answering. When she did, she began slowly, as if choosing her words carefully. "I think many people have a deciding moment in their lives when they struggle to make sense of their circumstances and question the purpose of life."

Tears rose in Lisa's eyes. She took a step closer to her aunt.

"I questioned whether I could even go on."

"Y-You wanted to give up?" Lisa said.

"Sadly, yes. At that point, I had no one I could turn to. After all, I hadn't talked to my parents in years. They never really accepted Frank or our marriage. In the end, it all added up to one thing—I missed my husband and was plagued with an overwhelming loneliness." She let the admission hang in the air before continuing.

"Lisa, we all have our own struggles in life. God uses those struggles to build us up and strengthen us. Not to hurt or punish us. He is the answer to our troubles. He was there for me. He's there for you, Lisa. Sometimes, we just need help getting there, and He brings someone unexpected into our lives to remind us of that and to help us through."

"Like Mike?" Lisa said.

A gentle smile passed over Aunt Jane's face. She nodded. "I was still going to church, but I hadn't truly expressed my feelings of total help-lessness to myself, or to God for that matter. I was prepared to be alone for the rest of my life. Then Mike started giving me special attention."

"I still don't understand."

"I didn't either, at first. I was afraid I was using my relationship with Mike as a substitute for the emptiness I felt after losing Frank."

"So you don't really love Mike?"

"No, that's not what I said. You didn't let me finish." She took a deep breath, then continued. "Lisa, sweetheart, I know this is difficult, but try to understand. This isn't about Mike—not really. Yes, I craved human companionship; that's natural, God made us that way. But that will never fill the void in our hearts. Only God can provide that. My point is, I had to find my comfort and completeness in God first." She leaned forward and picked a few flowers.

"So?"

"So I finally realized the only way to truly honor Frank was to move on, using the opportunity to grow stronger in my love for God. Only then could I be complete and happy. Only then was I ready to find love with someone else."

"I understand what you are feeling," Aunt Jane continued, "but you need to understand, I am never going to forget your uncle; he will be in my heart until the day we are reunited in heaven. Nevertheless, that doesn't mean I should stop living a new and happy life. God still has plans for me. You may not believe or understand it yet, but God has great plans for you too. You just haven't seen it yet." She handed one of the flowers to Lisa. "But you will if only you trust Him."

Her aunt's declaration of faith caught Lisa off guard. She'd known her aunt and uncle were religious, but this was different. Aunt Jane genuinely believed God was her reason for living, and Lisa's too. And she believed Lisa had a promising future.

But what did God have to do with it? Couldn't she do it on her own? She twirled the flower between her fingers as she tried to wrap her mind around everything her aunt had said.

"Well," Aunt Jane said. "We should probably go." The two linked arms as they made their way back to the car.

"Thanks for sharing this place, Aunt Jane. I'll admit; it helps to know you still think of Uncle Frank."

"I thought it might. I'm really happy I could share it with you."

You would be so proud, Frank. Your niece is trying to find her way; despite every roadblock the Devil puts in her path.

"No time for tears," Jane whispered, wiping a tear from her eyes.

"What?" Lisa turned to her.

"Oh, sorry. I didn't mean to say that out loud. I was just thinking, you've come so far in the last couple of days. Uncle Frank would be so proud of you. You know that, right?"

"Thanks, Aunt Jane. I hope you're right, but I really miss hearing him say it."

Jane wrapped her left arm around Lisa's shoulder and gave it a gentle squeeze. Why hadn't she thought of this before? They needed this time together, not only to renew the closeness they once shared but also to remind Lisa that, despite the changes happening with her and Mike, her home would always be a soft place for her to fall.

CHAPTER 11

Scott sat at the kitchen table eating a peanut butter sandwich his mother had made. Two days had passed, and still no word from Lisa. He was beginning to fear the worst. Keeping his accident a secret from her had been too much, and he had created the exact situation he'd hoped to avoid—facing her disapproval and potentially her rejection. Not that he blamed her. After all, she'd had enough to deal with in the past two years. Now he was just another disappointment in her life. She must have felt so betrayed. Anyone in her situation would have. Why couldn't he have seen that before and avoided this? He should have been in touch with her more. I should have let her know what was happening.

"It's all my fault."

"What's all your fault?" His mom stopped washing dishes and turned from the kitchen sink.

"Lisa hasn't called me back since she was here. I think I really messed up, springing everything on her like that."

"Well, I'm sorry, son, but can you blame her? She's going to need some time. I'm sure it's difficult for her with everything else she's been through." She walked to the table and picked up his now empty plate. "This isn't about how you feel, this is about Lisa."

His mother always had a unique way of getting past all the mess and confusion and getting down to the real issue—to speaking the truth in love. Today was no exception.

Scott was worried about Lisa; she was troubled. But he was equally concerned about how his actions would impact their future friendship.

"Don't worry about the future, Scott. Focus on the present and allow God to work in this situation. That's the only way you can really help her."

"I know; it's just so hard sometimes."

"You need to have faith, sweetheart. God is moving in ways you may not understand; I'm sure of that."

"I sure hope you're right, Mom," Scott said, wheeling his chair down the hall and into his bedroom.

Shutting his door behind him, Scott sent up a quick prayer.

God, forgive me. This is Lisa's life we're talking about, and I'm worried about myself. I don't want to lose Lisa; I want her in my life, even if it's only as a friend.

Since his accident, he'd prayed for an opportunity like this to present itself, a chance to test the authenticity of his walk with the Lord, but he'd buckled under the pressure. He had told Lisa about his accident, yes. But he'd left out the most important part—how God used the experience to draw him closer to Himself.

And that wasn't all he'd left out. There were more than a few key details about the accident he'd not shared. Details that better explained his new outlook. He'd wanted to make sure she was ready to hear it all, not just about his accident but also about the God who had changed his life. At least, that's what he'd told himself. Was it true? Or had he just been afraid of what she'd think of him?

For one thing, she might look at him differently if she realized it had taken the accident to make him realize the dangerous path he was heading down. He'd been so oblivious back then, taking everything in life for granted. Not anymore. Being in a wheelchair had given him a unique opportunity to see things from a different perspective. It had also given him a second chance to do things right. Over time, he'd learned the importance of his relationship with his family and, more importantly, his relationship with God.

He only hoped she'd see the change all of this had made in his life. That would be a step in the right direction. Scott bowed his head.

What have I done, Lord? I missed a wonderful opportunity to share your love with Lisa, all because of my pride. I leaned on my understanding and forgot to acknowledge you in the process.

He shook his head with regret. If given another chance, he would do it differently.

If only . . .

Scott's cell phone buzzed several times before he was able to find it under the books piled on his desk.

"Hello?"

"Scott. Hi. It's Lisa. I'm glad I reached you."

Lisa's sweet voice came through like a song.

"Lisa, I'm so glad you called. You had me worried." His heart quickened as relief flooded his body. *Thank You, Lord, I guess you're not through with me yet.*

"Worried? Why would you be worried?"

"Well, I hadn't heard from you for a couple of days. A lot of my friends really couldn't deal with seeing me like this after my accident, so . . . I was afraid maybe you felt the same."

"Scott, you should know better. We've been friends forever, and I plan on keeping it that way. You're not getting rid of me so easily."

"I'm glad to hear that."

"Actually, I really enjoyed our visit, and I've been thinking a lot about what you said. But there's one thing I'm curious about . . ."

"What's that?"

"It's . . . It's the way you've changed. You seem—I don't know—less . . ." she paused. "Just different from how you used to be. The last time I saw you, you were pretty focused on all you had going on, you know? All your plans and stuff."

Scott couldn't believe his ears. Not only had she noticed his change, but also she had opened the door for him to share the true reason for it. He shot up a silent prayer of thanks.

"So, what's that all about? What's your secret?"

"As much as I'd like to take the credit for the changes, I can't. I have someone bigger to thank for that. Someone who has completely changed my life."

"Let me guess, God?"

"How'd you know I was going to say that?"

"Let's just say you're not the only one who thinks God is the solution to all my problems." Lisa laughed. "Aunt Jane does too."

"Well, your aunt is right. But, ultimately, it's a decision everyone has to make for themselves." Scott hesitated for a moment. "Listen, I don't feel comfortable doing this over the phone. Why don't I come over on Monday so we can talk face to face?"

Scott waited anxiously for an answer. On the one hand, it was important to seize every opportunity when it came to witnessing. But the situation was complicated and doing it over the phone made it seem so impersonal. He had to put this in God's hands. God would work in Lisa's heart and prepare her. For Lisa to understand the impact of his transformation, she had to see the repentance in his heart as he told her his story. The whole story.

"Sure. I should be around if Aunt Jane doesn't have us shopping for wedding dresses." Lisa chuckled. "Turns out, she's getting engaged!"

"What?"

"Yeah, apparently she's in love again. Some guy she met at church. Mike. He seems all right, but, if I'm honest, I'm still not convinced."

Lisa hung up the phone, stunned. For as long as she'd known him, she'd never seen Scott like this. Even when they were young, he'd always been so confident and self-sufficient. So sure of himself and his future. Now, even though he no longer had any clear direction and he was no longer the center of attention, he still seemed so sure of himself. But this time it was different. Despite the change in his circumstances, it was like he was drawing strength from something beyond himself. He seemed almost . . . humble. There was so much Lisa had always liked about Scott, but this was new, the idea of being happy despite her circumstances, and she found it compelling. Growing up, Lisa had always believed her parents were responsible for her happiness. But seeing Scott struggle to make the best out of his circumstances and yet still find happiness proved she'd been wrong. Her parents couldn't make her happy. That was her job. Being happy was a conscious choice; a choice to remain satisfied with whatever twists and turns came her way. Scott had proved that. And while she might not be able to fix the problems at home, she still had the choice to be happy. And who knows? If she could make that change in her own life and find the happiness she'd been missing, maybe her parents would see it too.

Her parents!

She hadn't contacted them once since she sent the text when she arrived at Aunt Jane's saying, "I've arrived! Call you later." Amid all the chaos, she had forgotten to call as promised. Not that it made a difference. They'd probably been so glad to be free of her drama, they hadn't missed her.

Give them a break. They have their own problems. They still deserve respect.

It was true. And as the chiding inside grew stronger, going from her brain and into the depths of her heart, she was faced with a serious question: Why had she left her family? To escape her pain and find her own way? But didn't love mean sticking it out in tough times and not pushing people away? Scott had made that choice at first, keeping his distance and keeping her in the dark about what he was going through, and their relationship had suffered the consequences. She'd felt hurt and betrayed. That wasn't love or respect.

Her decision was set. She'd be the bigger person this time and apologize; that way, the lines of communication would remain open, and in her own small way, her parents would know she cared. The rest would be up to them.

Lisa sat at the kitchen table with Aunt Jane, enjoying a bowl of ice cream and studying her science textbook, when Aunt Jane's phone buzzed on the kitchen counter.

Probably Mike.

Aunt Jane rose from the table to get it, but Lisa continued to study, hoping her aunt would take the call to the other room.

"Well, hello . . ." The conversation faded as Aunt Jane walked into the living room to continue her conversation. After several minutes, she returned to the kitchen and approached Lisa.

"Lisa, it's your mom. Do you want to say hello?"

Well, here goes.

"Okay."

Lisa stood and accepted the phone. "Hey, Mom. I've been meaning to call you."

As Lisa paced the length of the kitchen, Aunt Jane slipped quietly out of the room.

"Yes, Mom, of course. I've already started studying. I will . . . okay. Thanks. I will . . . Okay, but I need to say something before you go." Lisa quickly gathered her courage, then poured it all out quickly, before she could change her mind. "I'm sorry, Mom. For everything. I know my bad grades and fighting with you guys didn't help, and I know we're all still grieving, and that you and Dad are having some problems, but we're still a family." Lisa stopped to catch her breath. For the first time in a long time, she wasn't giving in to what felt good at the moment or letting her negative emotions take control of her. It wasn't easy, but she was choosing to do what was right.

She waited, hoping for an appreciative response.

"Well, okay," her mother said. "We miss you too, but enjoy your time with your aunt."

"I miss you too. All right. I'll talk to you later, then. Bye, Mom." Lisa hung up the phone.

"That sounded like it went well," Aunt Jane said, coming up behind and hugging her.

"It did, but . . ."

"But what? You took an important step today, honey. You took responsibility for yourself and your actions."

"I guess. But it's like she didn't even hear me." Lisa dropped the cell phone on the kitchen table. "She didn't have anything to say, even after I apologized."

"Honey, she probably didn't know what to say after your impressive speech. Listen, things won't necessarily change overnight, but they've already started . . . and you started them. I'm so proud of you."

"From your mouth to God's ears." Lisa chuckled, then shrugged.

"Don't you worry, honey. That's already been taken care of."

Scott glanced at his watch. A little after ten p.m. He'd just finished reviewing Bible verses to share with Lisa when reality hit him head-on. His initial conversation with her had gone well. Seeds had been planted. But he knew sharing the truth about his accident would be challenging. However, creating a correlation between it and Lisa's current circumstances would be even more complicated. After all, seeing God moving in his life was one thing, but getting Lisa to let God into her own—that would take a miracle!

Oh, but I am the God of miracles, Scott . . . Haven't you realized that yet?

The gentle pleading of Acts 15:8 stopped Scott cold: *God, who knows the heart, showed that he accepted them by giving the Holy Spirit to them, just as he did to us.*

He was doing it again, forgetting about God's power, and taking on all the responsibility for Lisa's spiritual life.

"Forgive me, Lord. Not my will, but Yours be done."

He found himself saying that prayer a lot lately. In a small way, those simple words served as a constant reminder of how far he still had to go. He was falling for the girl, but that couldn't overshadow his goal to share his faith with her. That's what it was all about, right? The important thing now was for Lisa to recognize and acknowledge her need for God in her life. God was in charge of that. He could only do his part. The problem was: Would she listen to him? He'd let her down, just like so many others in her life. As unnerving as it was, that reality kept him focused on the truth: he wasn't the one Lisa should be counting on, Jesus was. The sooner she learned that, the better off they'd both be.

Scott sighed. He was doing it again. Even as he tried to keep the focus where it belonged, he found himself falling into the same old trap again. The trap of self. The truth was: He liked the idea of being someone's knight in shining armor.

"Get over yourself," he whispered.

With that, his mission became incredibly clear: He would have to shift the focus from what he wanted to say to letting the Holy Spirit direct him. God would never fail Lisa, and without a doubt, He would be the best friend she could ever have.

Let's just hope she listens to my story long enough to realize it.

CHAPTER 12

The house was unusually quiet when Lisa woke Sunday morning. It was almost ten; surely Aunt Jane wasn't still sleeping.

Shuffling downstairs to the kitchen, she found the coffee carafe and filled it with water. This was the first morning Aunt Jane hadn't been waiting for her with freshly brewed coffee and a hot breakfast, reading her Bible at the table.

Oh, that's right! Aunt Jane had told her she'd be leaving early for church on Sunday. Well, she'd have to get her own breakfast this morning. But she was used to that—at home, she always took care of herself, cooking her own breakfast and packing her lunches. Once or twice a week, she would even make dinner for herself and Dad while Mom was at work. She wasn't a great cook, but she could follow the directions on a box of mac-and-cheese or make a grilled cheese sandwich. Her father always appreciated the meals she made, but they never really talked while they ate, and her dad always disappeared to the garage as soon as he'd scarfed his down.

She sat at the table to wait for the coffee to brew and found a note from Aunt Jane scribbled on a flowery pad of paper:

Lisa, I've gone to church and will be back before one. This would be a suitable time to hit the books. I'll bring lunch back. Looking forward to the day with you.

"Woohoo," Lisa said, sarcastically. "I get to spend the morning studying."

Aunt Jane returned home just after one, as promised, with carryout from a local Amish restaurant. Lisa could smell the chicken and dumplings even through the paper bag. Her mouth salivated.

"Oh, thanks, Aunt Jane." She quickly gathered up her books and stacked them on the nearby counter.

Aunt Jane began removing the containers of food from the bag. "Would you get the plates and silverware for us?"

Lisa collected two blue Delft plates, silverware, and napkins from the kitchen cupboard. They sat together at the table, and Aunt Jane reached out for Lisa's hand as she bowed her head to pray. "Thank you, Lord, for this food and for this special time you have given me to share with my niece. Amen." It was a short prayer, but the fact her aunt had included her in it was touching.

Lisa had forgotten how amazing the local Amish cuisine was and devoured it quicker than usual, while Aunt Jane summarized the morning's sermon. She found it interesting that the sermon had been about Jesus choosing his disciples. He chose fishermen and a tax collector, and they just left everything to follow Him. After telling Lisa about the service, the singing, and her chat with her best friend Addie, Aunt Jane casually mentioned that Mike had not been there and that he was visiting his children in Michigan over the weekend.

Lisa rolled her eyes internally. *Of course she'd mention him.*

Once they'd eaten every last morsel of food, Lisa picked up their plates and silverware and placed them in the sink. "I'll wash the dishes," she said. "After all, you did the cooking."

Aunt Jane laughed. "That's okay, Lisa, I'll do the dishes, such as they are." She winked. "You can do some more studying."

"Oh geez, thanks, Aunt Jane!"

While Aunt Jane washed dishes and disposed of the containers and bag, Lisa glossed over several pages in her science book. But her mind wasn't on studying. She was thinking about what Aunt Jane had said when they were in the field of wildflowers, and she realized she had a point. Since her arrival, she had done her best to ignore the stirrings deep within her heart, but lately, she'd not only had the courage to apologize to her mother and to try to understand her aunt's new relationship, but she'd also begun to find her self-confidence once again. More than that, she finally felt hopeful that her life could change for the better.

"One thing still baffles me, though," Lisa said, closing her science book and turning her chair to look directly at her aunt. "Why?"

"Why what?" Her aunt said with a puzzled expression.

"Why now? Why would God want to change my life now? Why not when Ryan was alive?"

"I'm sorry, sweetheart, only God knows the answer to that sort of question. Perhaps we aren't ready to accept Him. You know, sometimes it takes a tragedy to open our hearts to Him, for us to become vulnerable. To teach us what's really important in life. Look at Scott, for instance. His life seemed great. Everything was going well by all human standards, but God wasn't a priority for him. The accident changed that. But despite what would be considered a tragedy by the world's account, he seems to have made peace with it. It couldn't have been easy."

Lisa's mind drifted back to their visit. He'd been so attentive and supportive, and, yes, she'd seen a vulnerable side of him as well. He'd told her about the accident and how God had changed him. Although it was clear his faith now played an important role in his life, he hadn't pressured her; he'd simply shared his personal experience, allowing her to draw her own conclusions. More importantly, he'd been encouraging, making her feel like she was important to him.

"That's true," Lisa said, "but I can't help wondering if it's more than that."

"I'm not sure I understand."

"Oh, it's probably nothing. It's just . . . call me crazy, but I could almost swear Scott has feelings for me."

"Of course he cares for you, Lisa. You two have been friends a long time."

She pursed her lips. "That's not exactly what I meant, and you know it."

Aunt Jane chuckled. "All right, you got me there." She crossed the kitchen and sat next to her. "But . . ."

"What?" Lisa held her breath, waiting for the other shoe to drop.

"But I'm just not sure now is the time for you two to start a romantic relationship. Getting involved could complicate things for both of you, and if you're not careful, it could cloud your judgment."

"Cloud my judgment?" Lisa stifled a laugh. "What about you and Mike? Isn't that the same thing? I mean, weren't you still mourning Uncle Frank when you guys started dating?"

"No, our situations are totally different, and I would appreciate you being more respectful, Lisa." She paused and laid a hand on her arm. "Listen, I'm a lot older than you; I have more experience when it comes to love. It's quite different. I'm not trying to make you feel bad, Lisa. I just want to protect you from getting hurt. I've lived a bit longer than you, and I know a few more things."

Heat rose through Lisa's cheeks. She shook her head and pushed herself to her feet. "Whatever, Aunt Jane! You just don't understand."

There was nothing more to say—clearly, they had opposing views on the subject. She snatched her science book from the table, turned on her heels, and stormed to her bedroom.

Sunday evening, Scott sat at his desk reading his Bible. Tomorrow, he would see Lisa. Was he ready? He'd asked himself that a lot lately. Telling her the full truth about his accident would be hard enough. But that wasn't all he'd been called to do, and he had to put Lisa's spiritual condition before his personal comfort. He wanted to stand firm; he'd been called to be a witness for Christ, and this would be a test of that commitment.

A gentle reminder from Luke 10:2 came to mind: *The harvest is plentiful, but the workers are few.*

Not too long ago, he was one of those followers Jesus talked about in Matthew, one who believed but kept the good news of his faith to himself, unwilling and incapable of seeing the world for the mission field it really was. But all of that changed the day he recommitted his life to Christ. He couldn't risk losing focus again, not when Lisa's eternal life was at stake. It was too important, and he cared about her too much to allow that to happen.

Things will be different this time.
God willing, he'd be ready.

"Lisa, my Monday Ladies' Bible Study is at eleven this morning, but I can skip it if you want me to."

Perfect! Now Scott and I can talk privately.

"No, I'll be fine."

With last night's disagreement behind them, Lisa was focused on Scott and finding out if he saw her as more than just a friend. Maybe she could get him to tell her what he was keeping from her about the accident too. How bad could it really be?

Lisa took her time preparing for Scott's visit. After a hot shower, she dressed in a pale blue blouse and dark blue jeans. Standing in front of the mirror, she dabbed concealer under her deep brown eyes and decided to pull her hair up into a ponytail. She finished it off with a blue dotted scarf. Lastly, she applied a light pink lip-gloss to her lips, and then took a final look before heading downstairs.

He'd be there any minute.

CHAPTER 13

"Are you sure you can manage on your own, Scott?" his mom asked as she wheeled his chair next to the open passenger car door.

Scott smiled. "Yes, Mom. I've got to learn to do this stuff on my own, don't I?"

She locked the chair in place. "Okay, well, call me when you're ready to be picked up."

"Thanks, Mom." Scott carefully placed his arms on the armrests and lifted himself into the chair. Lifting his legs one at a time, he placed them on the footrests and backed away from the car. He swung the door closed, and, moments later, his mom was heading down the driveway as he wheeled himself toward the back porch.

That's when it all went terribly wrong.

"Hey Lisa, it's me!" he called through the kitchen screen door. "Could you come outside for a minute? I could really use a hand."

Lisa appeared in the doorway and looked down to where he lay on the porch steps next to his upside-down chair.

"Oh my gosh, are you okay?" She flew down the stairs toward him.

"I'm fine. Just a wounded pride."

Lisa laughed, covering her mouth with her hand. "Quite a predicament you've gotten yourself into." She tipped the chair right side up and pushed it to the top of the porch while Scott scooted up the remaining step. He smiled up at her. "Well, I'm here!"

"Thanks, Lisa. I don't know what I'd have done without you." Scott sat next to her at the kitchen table, enjoying the fresh lemonade she'd prepared

for them. "You'd think I would've remembered those stairs before I came."
He laughed.

"How'd you get here anyway?"

"My mom dropped me off."

"Well, good thing I was here to rescue you." Lisa peered over her glass
and directly into his eyes.

"Yeah, a very good thing."

A few minutes later, Scott remembered why he was there. He had been
so caught up with his feelings for Lisa—the warmth in her brown eyes and
wondering what it would be like to kiss her—that he'd almost forgotten he
had a job to do.

"Lisa, I really need to apologize."

"Scott, please. We've been through this already. You don't need to."

"That would be true if I'd told you the complete truth from the beginning." Scott looked straight at her and steadied himself. This wasn't going
to be easy.

Lisa reached across the table and gently touched his hand. "So let's start
fresh. We've both made mistakes, but it doesn't matter now."

"That's my point, Lisa," he said, quickly pulling his hand away. "It
does make a difference; it makes all the difference in the world!"

"Scott, I'm sorry. I didn't mean to upset you . . ."

He shook his head. "I'm not upset. Not with you anyway. I'm mad at
myself for waiting this long to come clean about everything. The truth is,
I wasn't ready."

Lisa tilted her head. "I don't understand. Ready for what?"

"Ready to admit to everyone—including myself—that I've been
a fraud."

"I still don't understand. What are you trying to say, Scott? Just
tell me."

"Lisa, after the accident, I was forced to take a good look at myself,
and I didn't like what I saw."

"Well, you're better than me. I'd have been too angry for any sort of
self-reflection."

"At first, I was. My whole life had been stripped away from me. I was devastated."

"You seem okay now, though, right?"

Scott chuckled. "I know my accepting all this now may make me seem like a saint or something, but, in reality, it's the complete opposite. Because there's something else I haven't told you."

"Which is?"

Scott took a deep breath. He'd spent a lot of time thinking about what he would say when he had this talk with Lisa. Now that he'd set the ball in motion . . . he stopped to take a drink of his lemonade. This next part was going to be hard.

"Scott? What is it you aren't telling me?"

He swallowed hard. "That it was my own bad decisions that caused the accident."

Lisa's brows pulled together. "Wait a minute. You're not making any sense. Are you saying you lied to me about what happened before?"

Her words stabbed deeply at his heart. If only he could continue to hide the truth. But he was done living lies. It was time to walk in the light.

"Like I told you before, we were all playing basketball at the school. That part was true. Then one of the guys came with a case of beer, and—"

"Wait." Lisa's eyes opened wide. "Are you telling me you were drinking and driving?"

He braced himself. "Yes."

Lisa sat back in her seat. She looked as if the air had been sucked out of her. "Scott . . . how could you? Don't you know you could've been killed. You could have killed someone else, Scott."

Lord, is this right? Why tell her the truth just to have her hate me in the end? What kind of witness will I be then?

The gentle reassurance from Proverbs 3:5 came just in time:

Be anxious for nothing, my son. Trust in Me.

Telling Lisa the truth might destroy any illusions she had of him, any idea of him being perfect. But that was just it—he wasn't. No one was. And that was exactly what she needed to accept before she could let go of the hurt others had caused her. And it was what she needed to understand to fully comprehend the significance of Jesus in her life.

Lisa couldn't believe what she was hearing. Drinking? Enough to crash his car and end up in a wheelchair? Wasn't he smarter than that? Only two months before, two of her classmates had been killed in an accident after drinking at a school dance. The twisted remains of their car had been parked in front of the school and adorned with photographs and flowers as a visual reminder of the dangers of drinking and driving. But Scott? She just couldn't believe he would be so stupid. This wasn't the way he'd portrayed himself.

Scott wheeled his chair closer to Lisa's. "I'm so sorry. I should have told you sooner. I know this wasn't what you were expecting, but it's the truth. And if there's anything I've learned, it's that the truth is going to come out one way or another. The drinking . . . it had really become a problem for me."

"So you drank often then? Like . . . how often?"

Scott lowered his head. "I'm not perfect, Lisa. I never claimed to be. I have my weaknesses just like everyone else."

"Stop making excuses, Scott!" Lisa stood and pushed past him. She couldn't listen anymore. She stood at the back door and stared at the orchard beyond the back lawn, promising herself that no matter how much it hurt, she wouldn't cry. She hurt for Scott, yes, and she hurt for their relationship, but mostly she was angry he'd kept so much from her. If he weren't the person he'd pretended to be, would she ever be able to trust him again?

"I'm not trying to make excuses, Lisa. It's not like that." He rolled his wheelchair behind her.

"Really?" she said, keeping her eyes locked on the trees. "How is it then? Explain it to me."

"I'm just trying to tell you what happened. I had a big problem, and it wasn't something I wanted to make public. Not just because of how it would affect me, but because of my family too."

Lisa swung around to face him. "But I'm not just anyone, Scott! I thought we were friends. You're saying I'd—what?—reject you? Tell the whole town?"

"Not at all. Please hear me out." Scott's eyes pleaded with her, and he reached out and grabbed the tips of her fingers. "If our friendship means anything to you, please, just listen."

"Fine, I'll listen. But I really have nothing to say right now." Lisa brushed past Scott, walked to the table, and sat. He'd made a good point. If she valued their friendship at all, she would hear him out. She could give him that much. Taking a deep breath, she tried to calm herself and prepared to listen and not react.

Scott made his way back and pulled his chair next to hers.

"Even now, I wonder if thinking of those around me would have changed anything. I really don't know. Maybe not."

"You had everything going for you, though. Why? I just don't understand why?"

"Let me start from the beginning." He clasped his hands together and took a deep breath before starting again. "Lisa, I know my life looked great on the outside. Between the scholarships and the chance for all those sponsorships, I felt like nothing could go wrong. I was invincible."

"It was what you always dreamed about, right?"

"Sure. It was all I cared about, if I'm honest. I mean, the things that were being offered to me could've changed my whole future. Even my family's future. But that's the thing—the pressure to perform became too much. Before long, I felt like I couldn't do it anymore. The expectations, the attention—none of it. It was all too much."

"But you had your parents. Didn't they support you?"

"Sure, they did. At first, they saw all the opportunities as a unique gift from God. But they did have some concerns. For one, they were afraid I'd be affected academically. It took some convincing, but they finally agreed to let me move forward. The money would really help with my plans for college."

"In the beginning, I really thrived. I managed my grades, the money helped my family, and they were proud of me. But it didn't take long before the pressure became too much. My grades began to suffer, and they became concerned. Looking back, I realize they were right."

"So what happened?"

Scott shrugged. "I let the fame go to my head. I spent more time out in the gym practicing my free throws than I did on my homework; as a result, my grades dropped, and I almost got kicked off the team. I was under so much pressure. With the popularity came new friends . . . and maybe not the best of friends. They always had beer with them. Always. Every day. At first, I avoided it. But one day, I gave in. After that first drink, all the things that had been weighing on me suddenly felt a lot less heavy."

"My parents figured things out pretty quickly. Things got really bad at home. They fought about it a lot. Mom wanted to pull the plug on the whole thing, playing sports, the sponsorships, everything. But Dad thought I'd work it out. Like it was just a phase or something. But for me . . . I was the star, and no one could tell me otherwise. In my mind, I'd proven myself as a man, making money, helping the family. It was my life, you know?"

"I stopped going to church pretty early on. I was breaking curfew and hanging out with a pretty rough crowd. And, yes, to answer your question, drinking became a regular thing. I thought I knew what I was doing, but things were actually spiraling out of control."

"I had no idea. I never knew you felt like that." Lisa bit her lip to keep from crying. Scott's pain and regret were hard to ignore, and she felt them like they were her own.

"That's exactly how I wanted it. The last thing I wanted was for anyone to know what was really going on. I didn't want anyone's pity. Because then I'd have to face the truth about what I was becoming. Deep down, though, I was so ashamed of myself and my failure. But I wasn't ready to admit that, not even to myself."

Lisa's heart pounded in her chest. She was starting to understand. Like Scott, she'd struggled with similar feelings. She was never the star athlete he'd been, but she had found her self-worth in her academic achievements. So when those began to suffer, she felt the same shame and embarrassment he was describing. Was it possible she would have made the same mistakes he had, given the chance? Did she really have any right to judge him? Like kindred spirits, they'd both experienced the best and worst of what life had to offer. But Scott had grown stronger because of it. She'd only gotten worse.

"So what finally got through to you then? Was it the accident?"

"It was, but it was more than that. It was God. Coming face to face with death was a game-changer for sure; it changed everything. Not only physically but emotionally as well. It forced me to come to grips with my drinking and the fact that I had no one to blame for the accident but myself. That wasn't an easy thing to accept, and it didn't happen over-night. But with sports out of my life and my popularity fading, I had lots of time to get there."

Lisa shook her head. "So why are you telling me all of this now? It's obvi-ous you've changed; why not just go from here?"

"Because I care about you too much to damage our friendship by not being truthful. And because I hope the lessons I've learned can help you too. I don't want anything like that to happen to you."

"You think I'm going to start drinking or something?"

"Not necessarily. I just don't want you to make any of the same mis-takes I made. I want you to know there are better ways to fill the void. Take it from me."

"Lisa, I understand now that every decision I make has the poten-tial to change my life as well as those around me. I have to weigh every choice carefully and be willing to accept the consequences, whatever I decide. If I'd learned that earlier, the accident would've never happened."

"So what about your parents? How did they react?"

"Like you imagine—they were angry and hurt. Somehow, they felt responsible too. Don't get me wrong, they were grateful I survived and all, but the last thing they wanted was for their son to be in a wheelchair for the rest of his life." Scott's eyes had become moist, and he blinked a few times, then looked away.

"What did they do?"

"The only thing they could do," he said, looking back at her. "Pray. We were all praying. Little did I know, though, that we were praying for two different things. While I was focused on healing for my body, they were praying the accident would help me grow closer to God. I'll admit I had selfish motives at first. I thought if God saw that I was trying to change, He'd heal me, and things would return to normal. Like, He'd see I had learned my lesson and take away the consequences. When that didn't happen, I had to rethink my strategy."

Lisa understood completely. She'd always heard Jesus was a supernatural being who could perform miracles and intervene in the lives of humans if He chose to. She'd even tried praying for Ryan when he was sick. But, of course, he'd still died.

"That's one thing I've never been able to understand. People call Him 'the God of Miracles.' So why didn't He heal you?"

And why didn't he heal Ryan?

"He is. But He's so much more than that." A big smile lifted and brightened his face. "He's the best friend I've ever had."

"Scott, that doesn't make any sense."

"Oh, but it does. You see, for the very first time, I couldn't do anything to rectify my situation. Everything in this world that mattered had been taken away in a moment—or so I thought. During my recovery, I took time to read the Bible, and I discovered something. The accident may have taken my physical strength, but there was someone much stronger to get me through. I learned to depend on God for His strength and power. For the first time in my life, I found my true value and worth. And that's what enabled me to move forward."

"I'm really glad for you, Scott. Really, I am. And maybe it's right for you, but I really don't think it's for me."

"That's where you're wrong. God wants to give everyone a second chance at life. He's reaching out to you right now. Don't you get it? God brought you here. He knows you're searching for answers, answers that can only be found in Him."

"Whoa, slow down, Scott." She held up her hands. "I really don't know about all this . . ."

"I know, I know. I've given you a lot to think about. Lisa, just search your heart, and I'm sure God will show you the truth you've been looking for. Whatever happens, I'm here for you."

Scott reached into the pocket on the side of his chair and pulled out a book, then placed it on the table in front of her. Gold letters were pressed into the smooth black cover: HOLY BIBLE. She reached for it and ran her fingers over each letter.

"Okay," Lisa said softly. "Thanks."

She appreciated Scott sharing his story with her and finally being honest, but she still had so many questions. Too many things she couldn't just ignore.

CHAPTER 14

After dinner Monday night, Lisa helped clear the table and wash the dishes. "I think I'll do a little studying in my room and head to bed early tonight," she said, passing the last clean dish to Aunt Jane to be dried.

"Okay, honey." Aunt Jane placed the dried dish in the cupboard before turning to Lisa, her brows furrowed. "Are you okay? You've been unusually quiet tonight."

"Yeah, I'm okay. I'm just exhausted."

Lisa said goodnight, then trudged up the staircase to her room. She sat at the desk. Opening the top drawer, she pulled out the Bible Scott had given her.

Search your heart, and I'm sure God will show you the truth you've been looking for. The words made her angry when Scott said them, but they had echoed in her ears ever since.

For nearly thirty minutes, Lisa thumbed aimlessly through the pages. She'd been inspired by Scott's story and the peace he had despite the fact that he might never walk again. But who wouldn't be? Still, the more she thought about it, everything Scott had said about his faith and God made sense. She hadn't gotten very far trying to fix things on her own. In fact, she'd made them worse. On the other hand, Scott seemed to have the answers. He had found himself in an unbelievable situation, facing an uncertain future, yet he was still happy. Maybe there was something to this God thing after all.

Of course, he *had* kept his accident a secret for almost a year. And when he finally told her, he didn't even tell her the whole truth right away. How did that jive with everything else he said? If she couldn't trust him on one thing, could she really trust him on something as big as who God is and what He wanted for her life?

She picked up a framed picture from the desk and found Scott's face in the group. It had been taken the last time her whole family had come to the farm for the summer. The McCarthys, Sanchezes, and Mitchells had gotten together for their annual picnic, anxious to catch up on each other's lives. They were all so happy. Never in a million years could Lisa have foreseen what was to come.

At some point, Uncle Frank had set up his tripod and gathered everyone around the picnic table for a picture. As usual, he chose to stay in the background and document the day's activities for posterity. He always followed everyone around with his old Minolta camera, capturing the "simple moments"—a silly face made by one of the boys, a moment of affection between the other couples, or the families competing in a game of kickball. When Lisa asked why he took the job so seriously, he simply replied, "I'm making a memory for when my heart forgets to be grateful." That was Uncle Frank—he always found joy in the little things. For him, the best things in life were family and friends.

"Lisa, stop bothering your uncle and go play," her mother had scolded, "or come help us in the kitchen."

"Hush, Marion. She isn't buggin' me. Let her be," Frank called back playfully.

Her mother had only shaken her head in surrender and disappeared into the kitchen.

"Forgive your mother, sweetheart," Uncle Frank had said, squeezing her shoulder. "She doesn't remember what it's like to be your age. Curiosity is priceless. I love that about you. Never lose that, you hear me? It will lead you to remarkable things." He lifted his camera and snapped another picture.

She smiled. "Thanks, Uncle Frank."

If only she had known that would be their last time all together.

Lisa blinked back tears at the memory. Uncle Frank had been right. He had taken in every moment and stored it in his heart. That summer, they had all been so blissfully unaware of what the future held. She'd been no exception. She looked at the picture again and found herself.

What a fool she'd been, ditching her blue jeans and T-shirt to slip on that yellow sundress, all to impress Scott. All in the hopes of romance.

"I was so clueless," she whispered. Her efforts had been useless, and she had lost precious minutes with her family.

Back then, Scott was never interested in her that way, and he'd never been totally honest with her, even before the accident. She'd just been too infatuated to realize it back then. So where did that leave them now?

"Oh, Uncle Frank, if only you were here to give me some advice." She set the picture down and pushed her chair away from the desk, then slid the Bible back in the drawer.

"No, don't you leave me too!"

Lisa wrestled in her bed and woke to find herself kicking off the covers.

It had been just another dream . . . just a dream.

Her heart pounded in her chest. She was wide-awake now. She got up, slipped on her robe and slippers, and crept into the hallway. In the bathroom, she caught a glimpse of herself in the mirror while waiting for the water to warm. The dream had struck a nerve, and her face told the story. Pieces of the dream came back to her as she studied her reflection in the mirror.

She was dressed in a simple, A-line silk gown. Slowly, she glided down the church aisle into the arms of her one and only love—Scott. Ryan had been there, as the ring bearer, dressed like a miniature James Bond in a white tuxedo. And Aunt Jane and Uncle Frank too.

After the vows, the guests proceeded back to the McCarthy's, where a white tent lit by hundreds of twinkling lights and lavishly adorned with bouquets of wildflowers waited. Lisa stood with Scott, watching blissfully as the sun set over the horizon. Suddenly, a cold breeze caressed her cheek, causing her to shiver. A trumpet blew in the distance.

In a moment, the guests disappeared. Right into thin air, they were gone. Only her family remained, and they gathered around her.

"Why has everyone left?" she asked.

"They had to," Aunt Jane answered. "Didn't you hear the trumpet?"

"What?"

"God is calling His people home now, Lisa."

"She's right," Uncle Frank said, "and our time here is up." Without another word, he gathered Ryan in his arms and headed straight toward the sun. Within seconds, they were out of sight.

"Wait for me, honey," Aunt Jane said, following him.

"Whoa, you're leaving too?"

Aunt Jane stopped and turned back to her. "Honey, this old body isn't meant to last forever," she said, and then faded into the distance above.

"Scott?" Lisa said, reaching for his hand.

"Lisa, as much as I love you, I can't stay here. But this isn't goodbye if you believe in Jesus. It's only, 'See you later.'" He kissed her, then his hand slipped from her fingertips, and he was gone.

Lisa scrubbed vigorously at her face, as if to wash off the remnants of the dream, but the sound of her own voice pleading still echoed in her mind:

Don't you leave me too!

She'd asked him to stay, but it wasn't enough.

She wasn't enough.

When she was done in the bathroom, she grabbed the Bible from the desk drawer in her bedroom and walked down to the kitchen.

Taking a mug from the overhead cupboard, she flipped the switch to turn on the coffee maker and waited. What made Scott so sure she needed God in the first place? Yes, she'd made some mistakes. Still, she was getting back on track by taking responsibility for her part in the family dysfunction and doing what was necessary to make things right. Wasn't that enough? Furthermore, if Jesus cared as much as Scott said He did, where had he been up until now? These questions were fair and valid, and they needed to be addressed before she would even think about trusting in a God like that.

Lisa poured some coffee and took a seat at the table. Shivering, she pulled her bathrobe tighter against her. She hadn't realized how cold Aunt Jane's house was this early in the morning. Warming her hands on the hot mug, she enjoyed a full sip.

"*Mmmm.*" She smiled as the velvety liquid warmed her from the inside out. If only all of life were so easy to solve.

Outside, the sky had changed, darkness giving way to a lighter blue, as little streaks of pink and orange began to peek out over the horizon. It was going to be a beautiful day.

She shifted her focus from the mug of coffee to the Bible she had placed on the table. Scott had put a lot of stock into this book. What was the harm in doing a little research? It wasn't like it would turn her into a Christian overnight, but maybe it could help her understand better where Scott and Aunt Jane were coming from.

Pulling the book a bit closer, she examined it. Although the hardcover remained intact, its binding was loose, and some of the page edges were curled or folded over as if used as a bookmark. Apparently, this copy had seen Scott through many tough times—that much was obvious.

If only I knew where to start.

She flipped open the Bible and began thumbing through the pages, stopping when she reached the Psalms. She remembered the book from her family's brief attendance at Melissa's church. The psalms had always confused her. Moving through the chapters, she came to a page with several verses highlighted in yellow and Scott's handwriting alongside. As she read the verses, her breath caught in her chest.

When hard pressed, I cried to the Lord; he brought me into a spacious place. The Lord is with me; I will not be afraid. What can mere mortals do to me? The Lord is with me; he is my helper. I look in triumph over my enemies. It is better to take refuge in the Lord than to trust in humans. It is better to take refuge in the Lord.

Scott had written along the margins: *Maybe another reason for my accident, to get me to remember my weaknesses and refocus. Friends may desert me, but God never will.*

Underneath this note, he had also written two more references, Deuteronomy 31:6 and Matthew 28:28. Lisa found a table of contents in the front of the Bible and quickly found the first reference. It read: *Be strong and courageous. Do not be afraid or terrified because of them, for the Lord your God goes with you; he will never leave you nor forsake you.*

She found the next set of verses and read them too: *Therefore go and make disciples of all nations, baptizing them in the name of the Father and of the Son and of the Holy Spirit, and teaching them to obey everything I have commanded you. And surely, I am with you always, to the very end of the age.*

Lisa sat back and thought about what she'd read. The book was right about one thing— people will fail you. Almost everyone in her life sure had. Her parents were so busy fighting and consumed by their own grief that she had become practically invisible to them. Scott hadn't been there either. Not when she'd needed him. Even Aunt Jane hadn't been, not that she couldn't understand why.

Lisa took the last swig of coffee, and then walked to the sink to rinse out the cup. As she placed it in the sink, she noticed the light streaming through the windows all around, casting a golden glow on the kitchen floor. Suddenly her eyes felt weary. She made her way upstairs and returned to the comfort of her warm bed.

I'll think more about all this later.

Scott hadn't slept well. The conversation with Lisa had been hard. He'd awakened many times during the night to seek God in prayer. She had been so angry. He had lied, and she was hurt. But her pain and anger had been even worse than he'd expected.

She was still angry with him when he left her aunt's house. She had listened while he shared his testimony, but afterward, she didn't have much to say. She'd told him it would be better if he left and then went upstairs while he waited for his mother to pick him up, leaving him alone to replay the conversation. How heartbreaking it had been to watch Lisa's version of him crumble to the ground.

At least she knows the real me now.

Son, you know that was necessary. Lisa needed to see your weakness and humanity, the failure that brought you to Me. She will search for comfort and find I am the only true source of peace in this life. You've done your part; now let me do mine.

I know God, but how is she supposed to trust me after I've made her feel betrayed? How can she believe anything I've told her?

No, Scott. You've come too far in your faith to go there again. Now take it to the altar and leave it there.

Scott shook his head, his mind renewed. He wouldn't let doubt control his thoughts again. He had made every effort to lay down his concerns and requests to God daily, and he wasn't going to change that now. It wouldn't be easy, but he would relinquish his control and leave it to God.

As much as he wanted to share his faith and see a spiritual change in Lisa, there was another aspect to the situation that complicated things. He couldn't deny the physical attraction he was feeling. He had done his best to witness to her, all the while fighting to keep his mind off the scent of her hair and the softness of her peach lips . . .

Be careful, my son, that you do not fall into temptation.

The warning came rushing at him like a flood, quickly cooling his desires. Matthew 26:41: *Watch and pray so that you will not fall into temptation. The spirit is willing, but the flesh is weak.* For this too, he had no better answer than to turn to God in prayer.

Lord, please help me stay focused on leading Lisa to you and not on the feelings I have for her. Starting a relationship isn't a good idea. Not right now, anyway. She needs to find you first. Give me the strength to resist these feelings until it's the right time. And help us maintain our friendship through this process. Help me to stay strong."

He would have to be on guard against his own nature. He wanted to be there for Lisa and to continue to share his faith with her, but he'd have to set some boundaries. But how?

Where do I begin, Lord? Please show me.

Ask your dad. He will give you the answers you're looking for.

Of course! Why hadn't he thought of it before? His dad would certainly have some insight into how to remain friends without sending mixed signals. He would talk to him today. He needed someone much wiser than himself to help him move forward, and his dad was a smart choice.

CHAPTER 15

Lisa woke to the sound of raised voices downstairs.

Seconds later, the screen door to the kitchen slammed shut.

Lisa stood and slipped into her robe. Outside, a car roared to life. She walked to the window and peeked out through the curtains. Mike's sports car was backing down the drive. Lisa let the curtains fall back into place, then quickly threw on an oversized T-shirt and a pair of jeans. She found Aunt Jane downstairs at the kitchen table.

"Aunt Jane?" she said, but her aunt didn't move. Lisa slipped into one of the empty seats. Her eyes were red and moist.

"Aunt Jane, are you okay?"

Aunt Jane gave a weak smile. "Hi, honey. Did you sleep okay?"

"Don't worry about me. I heard yelling then I saw Mike driving away. What happened? Is everything okay?"

"Oh honey, I'm sorry you had to hear that. I didn't expect him to come over this morning, guns blazing." She folded her arms on the table in front of her. "I told Mike I think we need to slow things down. Let's just say he wasn't too happy about that."

Lisa's mouth dropped. She quickly covered it with her hand. "It wasn't because of me, was it? Aunt Jane, I'm so sorry. I know I could have been nicer to him . . . to both of you."

"Lisa, you don't need to pretend; I know you weren't in favor of our relationship. But, no, it wasn't you. I decided to turn down Mike's proposal for my own reasons. I'm way too old to be jumping into a marriage, and I need time to reevaluate things."

"What kinds of things?"

"I appreciate your concern, honey," Jane said, smiling, " but it's nothing for you to worry about. You have enough on your plate as it is." Her eyebrows suddenly lifted. "Speaking of plates, you must be hungry. Do you want me to make you something?" She jumped up from the table and crossed the room to the refrigerator.

Smooth one, Aunt Jane. Way to change the subject.

"No, but thanks. It'll be lunchtime before you know it. I think I'll just make myself some toast and reheat some coffee."

So Aunt Jane had refused Mike's proposal. Lisa felt awful. She never would have expected she'd feel this way. As much as she wanted to be happy about it, she wasn't. Aunt Jane seemed devastated, and, honestly, Mike really did seem like a good guy.

"I noticed the dirty mug in the sink this morning," Aunt Jane said, closing the refrigerator. "Couldn't sleep?"

"Not exactly," Lisa said. "Have you ever had a dream that made you question people's true intentions?"

"That's a curious question, Lisa. I'd have to think about it." Aunt Jane leaned her hip against the countertop and crossed her arms. "Psychologists will tell you that dreams are just your mind's way of making sense of every-day events and dealing with the emotions involved. But I believe God can use dreams as effectively as he did in biblical times, to encourage and warn us of challenges coming our way."

"Really? Do you really believe that?"

"Absolutely. When your Uncle Frank was overseas fighting in the war, there were days—even weeks—without a word from him. It was a difficult time, and after a while, I began doubting his love for me. I was so lonely, and I was struggling financially, and before long, I had no choice but to return to my parents' home. I'd often have dreams about him and wake in the middle of the night in fear for his safety. All I could do was pray." She paused as if remembering. "It wasn't until Frank returned home that he shared with me some of the close calls he'd experienced. I knew then, God heard my prayers, and I was certain He had kept your uncle safe."

"Wow!" Lisa had heard bits and pieces of her aunt and uncle's earlier years, but she'd never heard this part of their love story.

Aunt Jane settled back at the table across from her niece. "Those were some of the most difficult times in my life but also the most rewarding."

"Really? How so?"

"For one, the time apart allowed me to grow both emotionally and spiritually. You see, your uncle was my first love and my first real relationship, and I had unwittingly given him top billing in my life. I'd started to rely on him for every need."

"What changed?"

"Well, when he was off to war, I had no choice but to rely on God to provide for me. Time and time again, He proved faithful—whether through scripture, the support of family and friends, or one of Frank's letters arriving just when I really needed it. It's just like how He's done for you."

"Me?"

"Sure! Look at how God is working in your life to bring you closer to Him. You know, if your uncle were around, he'd tell you you're not here by coincidence. He didn't believe in those sorts of coincidences, and neither do I. Lisa, just think of all the things that had to happen for you to be sitting with me right here, right now. Not just the big things, but the small things too. From what you've told me, it didn't just begin with your decision to visit for the summer. It began with your difficulties at home, your parents fighting, your struggles at school, and even your sharing your talks with your friend Melissa. Then it continued when you arrived here and listened to Scott and me share our faith. Before this summer, you were always so closed off to the topic. But now, God is moving in your heart. I can see it. I just pray you remain open to learning more about Him."

Standing out on the front porch, Lisa waved as Aunt Jane's red convertible eased out of the driveway, its chrome wheels leaving clouds of dust in their wake.

Finally, she was alone.

Thankfully Aunt Jane hadn't argued when she declined the offer to go run some errands. She needed time alone—time to think and process everything. Aunt Jane had made some good points. Yes, this hadn't been the first time she'd been introduced to the Christian faith, but this was the first time she'd been open to the idea. After all, two of her closest friends and Aunt Jane had shared their faith experiences with her; their stories left her inspired and motivated to learn more about Christianity.

Maybe a short hike in the woods would do her some good; the fresh air always seemed to work its magic. Settled on the idea of a long walk, she made her way out the kitchen door and down the back porch steps, then eased her phone from her jeans pocket and found Aunt Jane's contact in her messaging app.

Going for a walk. Be back before dark. Don't worry!

She'd only walked a short distance before realizing she'd forgotten to lock the door. Retracing her steps, she slipped the key from its hiding place underneath the welcome mat just as her phone buzzed twice in reply.

Remember to lock the house up! I'll be a while. Be safe . . . or your mother will kill me! TTYL

Lisa laughed and fired off a quick reply. As much as Aunt Jane complained about modern technology, she'd certainly taken to it easily, making short order of learning all the text slang.

Slipping the phone back into her pocket, Lisa let out a sigh. It truly was a gorgeous day. The sun shone brightly above her in a cloudless blue sky, and a breeze blew at her face, winnowing gently through her brown locks and cooling the back of her neck. Perfect hiking weather.

At the edge of the woods, the scent of evergreen and wet leaves filled her nostrils. Stepping through the tree line, she felt the changing ground beneath her. The moisture of the mossy ground made finding good footing difficult at first. But, before long, she was deep into the forest, surrounded by towering pine trees and hidden from the sun.

She paused to breathe in the beauty of a tall, dark evergreen that stood majestically in front of her. Its deep, brown bark was scarred by both weather and age. It had suffered through harsh conditions, yet it stood as a testament to its endurance. Much like herself.

Lisa eased herself to the ground at the base of its massive trunk, her back pressed against its rough surface. Everyone made it look so easy, this thing they called "faith." They made it seem like such a wonderful place to be. She wanted that too. She wanted the peace they all seemed to have found. If only she could believe it.

She wrapped her arms around her knees and began to cry.

Out of the stillness of the forest, a voice whispered softly, "What's stopping you?"

Lisa's head shot up. She quickly swiped a hand across her eyes and scrambled to her feet. She scanned the surrounding forest, but saw no one—she was still alone.

I'm just exhausted. It's the wind blowing through the woods.

Still, maybe it was time to head back to the house.

Brushing the leaves from the back of her clothing, she took another look around. No, she had definitely heard something.

"Who's there?" she said.

Amidst the rustling of trees, a voice spoke clearly and strongly, asking again the curious question that addressed her doubts and fears: "What's stopping you?"

Lisa again looked around for the source of the voice. When she found none, she turned her face to the sky. "Please, God! It would be much easier if you showed yourself to me!"

"Come on, Lisa. You should know by now He doesn't always work like that."

Lisa swung around to the sound of the voice and found herself looking into the smiling face of a man. She stumbled backward.

"Wait!" he said, holding up his hands. And for some reason, she did.

"Sorry if I startled you," he said. "I just wanted to help."

Under normal circumstances, alone in the middle of the woods, she'd have been halfway back to the farm by now. But she couldn't seem to take her eyes off him. There was nothing particularly fascinating that she could see; he was average-sized, medium build, and his shoulder-length blonde hair was matted down against his forehead with sweat.

And despite being fairly good-looking, he looked a little disheveled and rough around the edges.

She struggled to recognize him, but he didn't look at all familiar. Still . . . how did he know her name?

"D-Do I know you?" Lisa finally asked.

"Not exactly. Friends call me Gabe." He stuck out his hand but did not step closer.

Lisa cautiously stepped forward to shake his hand. Despite the potential for danger, she felt instantly at ease around him, and as their fingers touched, a sense of peace coursed through her entire body.

"I'm sorry," she said. "I didn't mean to trespass. I didn't realize—"

"No, no, it's all right. I was just cutting wood for the family down the way, and I couldn't help but hear you crying—I wanted to make sure you were okay."

"But how did you know my name?"

He didn't answer but continued to look at her, his piercing blue eyes locked on hers.

Suddenly, a screech pierced the silence, jerking her attention away. She watched in awe as a bald eagle soared through an opening between the trees. She followed its path, its dark wings outstretched, as it weaved back and forth above her as if floating on the wind. The image of the great bird against the brightness of the sky was amazing. She was mesmerized. She watched until the bird was completely out of sight.

She turned back to the stranger. "But how did you—"

The man was gone.

Lisa quickly looked around in search of him. She jogged between the trees, looking in all directions, but he wasn't there. When she couldn't find him, she returned to the tree where she'd been sitting, completely baffled. She hadn't heard a thing. Not a single footstep as he walked away. And there was absolutely no physical sign of his ever being there. How could he have gotten away so quickly without leaving a trace?

Growing up, she had overheard Aunt Jane share stories with Uncle Frank about encounters with angels. She always said angels could come as strangers who seem to appear from nowhere and then disappear. What was it her aunt called it? Entertaining angels unaware? She had never believed these stories before, but she had to wonder . . .

No, that was ridiculous, right? Gabe couldn't have been an angel. She couldn't believe that.

Could she?

Lisa was out of breath by the time she made it to the house. Before she made it out of the forest, the sky had grown suddenly dark, and thunder rumbled overhead. She ran even faster than before, but the first waves of rain hit as she crossed the backyard, pelting her face with large drops.

She quickly turned the key to the back door and slipped into the warmth of the kitchen. Her mind raced. What had just happened? Who was Gabe? Why did she feel so . . . strange? She didn't know the answers, but the feeling inside of her was unlike any she'd ever felt before.

She pulled her cell from her back pocket and slipped into one of the kitchen chairs. Maybe Aunt Jane would be able to shed some light. She found her text thread with Aunt Jane and found she'd missed a text from her already:

Caught in storm. Hope u r home safe.

Lisa quickly thumbed out a response:

Made it just in time. Are you on your way home now?

Yes. Be back soon.

Okay, drive carefully. Boy, do I have a story to tell you. Do you know a guy around here named Gabe?

Around the farm? Can't think of anyone. Are you okay?

I'm okay . . . I think. I don't know. I just need to talk.

On my way. Talk soon.

CHAPTER 16

As much as Scott cherished "Family Fun Friday," his heart wasn't in it tonight. He couldn't stay focused on the card game he was playing with his two younger twin brothers. Instead, his brows furrowed over blue eyes with concern at the storm brewing outside the kitchen windows.

Devon slapped the table in front of them. "Scott, you playing or not?"

"Yeah, Scott, come on, man!" Marcel said.

"Hey, you two, leave your brother alone," their mother said. Your father will be home any minute with the pizza."

"Yeah!" Both boys flung their cards onto the table and started dancing in a circle.

As if on cue, Dad's boots stomped twice onto the welcome mat. "Did someone here order a pizza?"

Outside, the afternoon shower had gained momentum, turning into an all-out thunderstorm; heavy, black clouds quickly moved into position overhead, and the wind whipped the trees back and forth. Scott wheeled from the table to the window. He held back the curtain and watched in awe as rain and leaves banged against the window.

He hadn't heard a word from Lisa in days, and although he was determined to give her the space and time she needed, he couldn't get her off his mind. He didn't know why, but he awakened that morning with an overwhelming urge to pray for her and didn't know why.

What if she were in some kind of trouble? Could she have gone out for a walk? Was she lost? Hurt? She might have a hard time finding her way back in the storm. He sure hoped not, but he couldn't shake the feeling that something was up.

"It's really coming down out there!" His dad stepped into the kitchen and deposited the pizza boxes on the counter. "I could barely see the road in front of me. Thankfully, they were practically deserted."

His mom laughed. "I think most people have the good sense to stay inside during weather like this."

"Yes, but I'm not like most people," he said, grabbing a towel and wiping the water that dripped from his face and head. "You should know that by now." He wrapped his arms around her waist and kissed her.

His wife chuckled. "I know. But I married you anyway." She turned to her sons who were still bouncing around the kitchen together. "Come on, boys, stop fooling around, and help your father set the table, will you? That includes you, Scott."

"Yes, ma'am," Scott said. He let go of the curtain and smiled as he maneuvered through the kitchen helping his brothers with the plates and glasses of water for each of them. Until recently, he'd never really appreciated his parents' relationship. After over twenty-five years of marriage, they'd remained best friends by finding humor in the simplest moments. But they also took their relationship seriously, knowing time alone was important. They took their vows before the Lord seriously, committing to help each other grow spiritually both individually and as a couple. For this reason, they'd instituted a monthly date night to support and encourage each other. He wanted that with his wife someday.

When they'd all had enough to eat, Scott's mom stood and gathered the empty plates, then carried them to the sink. "Come on, boys. Let's give Scott and your dad some space, and I'll play a game of UNO with you before bed. There may even be some chocolate in it for you."

Instantly, the boys hopped off their seats and scurried behind their mother and out of the kitchen.

"So," his father began, "what's bothering you, son? You were awfully quiet at dinner. Is this about Lisa?"

Scott nodded.

"I thought you said you were going to give her some space. Wait for her to come to you."

"I was—I am. But this morning . . . I don't know; I've just had this feeling. Like, an overwhelming need to pray for her."

"So go ahead and pray for her, then."

"I am, but this weather . . . I just feel like something's wrong. Like maybe she's in danger or something."

"Scott, be serious. Lisa's with her aunt. I'm sure she's fine."

"I guess."

"Scott, I've got to be honest; I'm concerned for you, son. Ever since Lisa's arrival, you've changed. You spend your days moping around the house waiting for her to call. Your phone is practically glued to your hand. You like her, I get it—"

"Why do I sense a 'but' coming?"

"Well, frankly, you're slipping back into old habits. Worrying and anxious about things beyond your control. It's one thing to like Lisa and care about her well being; it's a totally different ballgame when you become consumed with worry for her and you stop trusting God. As difficult as this may be to hear, this is not about you."

His father was right. He'd spent more time thinking about Lisa in the past few days than he wanted to admit, and he'd forgotten to focus on God. Guilt washed over him as he swiveled his chair and headed to his room. "Thanks, Dad. I really appreciate your advice."

Aunt Jane walked to the kitchen sink and peered out the window. "I can't believe it's still raining so hard outside. My flowers will certainly appreciate it though." She turned to Lisa. "So, how's the studying going over here?"

"Fine, I guess." Lisa shut her Algebra book and turned to face her aunt. She'd been distracted from her studies, unable to focus for the last twenty minutes. This Gabe thing was driving her crazy. And it wasn't any better after talking with Aunt Jane. Just who was he? Could he really be an angel? Aunt Jane seemed to believe he was. When Lisa described Gabe to her, she said he sounded like the same man she met in her special spot in the woods after Uncle Frank died. And that man had also called himself Gabe.

"Aunt Jane, remember how we talked about Gabe, how he could have been an angel?"

"Yes, I remember Lisa. It was just a few hours ago." Her aunt chuckled. "I'm not that old."

"Right, sorry. Well, I was wondering why you never mentioned your experience with him before. Not even when we visited your special spot. It's a pretty amazing thing, you know, seeing an angel."

"Honestly, sweetheart, I never dreamed he would appear to you or anyone else, for that matter, or that I'd ever see him again."

"So you just kept it a secret and forgot about it? "

"No, not really. Every time I walk in those woods, I wonder if I'll see him again. It's just that . . . well, I wasn't sure anyone would believe me. They'd probably think I was a delusional old woman. Believe me, if I'd known you were going to have this experience, I would have told you."

"So, what did he say to you, anyway?" Lisa asked as her aunt placed a plate of cookies on the table and sat next to her at the table.

"Gabe reminded me of what my heart already knew but had forgotten since Frank's passing—that Jesus loves me and is watching over me. He acknowledged the pain in my loss here on earth but reiterated the glorious reality of heaven. Frank is with his Savior now; he feels nothing but joy."

"That's it?"

"I know that message means nothing to you now, but it meant the world to me at the time. I'd become despondent, questioning God's purpose in my life. My world revolved around Frank and our relationship, and now that was gone. I had to start over, learning to rely solely on Jesus as I had during the war."

"But why would an angel appear to me? I'm not even religious."

Aunt Jane shrugged. "That's not for me to say. God reaches out to us all in different ways and at various times. Just because you don't know or believe in Him doesn't mean He doesn't know you. The Bible tells us He knew us while we were still in our mother's womb. Maybe it's the only way He thought He could reach you, His way of letting you know He's real."

"Maybe. It's still kind of hard to believe, even though I was there."

"Jesus knows your heart and understands what you need better than anyone; after all, He is your Creator. He knows how much you need Him." Aunt Jane placed her hand over Lisa's.

"Gabe told me that God doesn't always work like that."

"Well, I certainly agree with that."

"What I still don't understand is why faith comes so easy to some and yet so hard for others. I mean, in the last few weeks, I've listened to several stories about how faith in God can change people's lives for the better—yours, Scott's, even Mike's. It's great, really. I want to believe; I really do but . . ."

"But?"

"Something's stopping me from taking the final step. Out there in the woods, I got so frustrated. I said it would be so much easier if He showed Himself to me; then I could believe."

"Sweetheart, don't you see? He did. That proves He's listening. Granted, He didn't exactly show himself in the way you'd expect, but He did send someone to you. He sent Gabe. Frankly, it's amazing!"

"But I don't understand what it means. What did Gabe mean by 'God doesn't always work like that'?"

"Well, there's the obvious meaning, of course," Aunt Jane began. "You know, how maybe you have in your mind things should go a certain way. Let's say with Scott, for instance. But God knows the bigger picture and how all the pieces fit together in the end. So what we think might be an answer to our prayers—what we really want to happen—might not actually be for our good. It might be the wrong puzzle piece for our lives."

"Then how are we supposed to know if He's answered our prayers?"

"That's a matter of faith."

Silence enveloped them as Lisa continued to contemplate the purpose and meaning of Gabe's visit. When the clock chimed eleven p.m., Aunt Jane eased herself up from her chair.

"My, where has the time gone? I should be heading to bed—considering I'm not a night owl like you," she said.

Aunt Jane said goodnight, then made her way toward the stairs. Halfway there, she stopped abruptly and turned back. "You know, talking to you is just like talking to your mom. You're always looking for the logical answers, but sometimes there just isn't one. You're growing up right before my eyes. Your uncle would be so proud, you know. You're on your way to amazing things."

Lisa smiled. "Thanks, Aunt Jane. Goodnight."

"Good night, Lisa." Jane said, "Don't forget to turn out the lights."

You're on your way to amazing things. Hadn't Uncle Frank said something along those lines the last time they spoke?

Yes, he had. She remembered it well.

After a few minutes, Lisa gathered her textbooks, stacked them neatly on the table, and headed to bed. Aunt Jane was right. It was late, and it had been a long day. Lisa climbed the stairs to her bedroom and closed the door. Aunt Jane had made some good points. Her heart had been opened a lot this summer. Not only had she listened to Scott's testimony without running away, but she'd also been able to recognize her part in her family's dysfunction and done her best to start making amends. And through many doubts, she'd even taken the first steps toward learning more about God.

CHAPTER 17

Scott wheeled himself back and forth in his room. He needed something to throw and fast. His father had made some good points earlier that evening. Since Lisa's arrival, he'd become preoccupied with her. He had come a long way since the accident, that was true; but he still struggled. He struggled with desires he knew weren't in God's will for his life. He struggled with depression. And even though he trusted God, there were times he was still angry about his circumstances. Had he really needed to lose his whole future to figure out what was important in life? If only he could go back and change his choices. Maybe he could do things right this time.

He still remembered well the day he first started accepting his new circumstances and became determined to work toward his new future. On that day, like pretty much every day since the accident, he'd slept in way past noon. Eventually, his mother came into his room to wake him:

"Time to get up, sleepyhead. It's a beautiful day outside."

"Leave me alone. I'm tired." Scott pulled the sheets tightly around him and a pillow over his head.

"Tired? That's hardly believable. It's almost one in the afternoon. I've been waiting all morning to help you get up, Scott, and I don't have all day."

"So."

"So, don't you think it's about time you get up? Maybe even start taking some responsibility for your life again? Scott, your brothers are worried about you. You don't want them to think you're dead in here, do you?"

"Let them think that. I don't care."

She walked over and pulled the cover back. "You know, this little attitude of yours is getting old. Now come on; it's time to get up."

"Huh?" Scott muttered from under his pillow.

"Don't play dumb. I know you heard me." She pulled the pillow from his head.

"Mom, come on! Can you just leave me alone?" He reached down without opening his eyes and pulled the covers back up to his chin.

"That's just it, Scott. I can't. I have to take care of you; I don't have a choice. And you're not the only one who needs me, you know. Your brothers need me too, and you expect me to be available whenever you feel good and ready to get up. That's just not how it works, Scott. And I really don't appreciate—"

"No one said you had to, Mom!"

"What other option do I have, son? Leave you here for days to sulk and lay in your mess? I don't think so." Again, she pulled the covers off of him.

"Leave me alone! Get out of here, will you?" He grabbed a throw pillow and tossed it in her direction, barely missing her head.

"No, I will not! You're getting up right now. You know what, son, you act as if you're the only person in the world suffering the consequences of your bad choices."

"I'm sorry, okay? How many times do I have to say that before you leave me alone?"

"Scott, I believe you're sorry. I really do. But we've all had to give up things."

"There's nothing I can do about that, Mom. I can't take it back. I wish I could. But I'm the one stuck here. I'm the one who's paralyzed. Not you, not Dad, and not Devon or Marcel. *Me!*"

"See, that's what I mean, Scott. All you think about is yourself and what you've lost. What about your father and me? We moved our family across town; we left the home we've loved and lived in for over twenty-two years. For you, Scotty! Your brothers too. They left their friends, left their pet goats, and gave up the life they were used to so you could have a better life. And they're worried about you, Scott." His mom took a deep breath. "We all are."

"Look, I really am sorry. You know that, right?" Scott said, finally pushing himself up on his elbow and looking at his mom.

"Don't tell me. Tell them," she said, pointing toward the open bedroom door. "Better yet, show us. Start putting some effort into building a new life for yourself. Be the best brother and son you can be."

"But what about this?" he said, gesturing to his leg. "I can't even—"

"What about it? So your legs don't work like they used to. You're still the same person to your brothers, Scott. You're still the same inside, aren't you? That's what matters. So you can't play basketball anymore. Your identity is not in what you do, it's in who you are and how you accept the difficult parts of life. Maybe you don't know what the future holds. The truth is, neither does anybody else. And, frankly, you're lucky to have a future at all."

Scott said nothing. There wasn't anything he could say. His mom was right, and he knew it.

That was the day things began to change. He became determined to start again. To find his true purpose in life. Before long, he had plunged into the Bible, searching for answers to why his accident happened; in the end, he had to accept the fact that his accident was a consequence of his own choices and sin, not a punishment from God. He was alive only by the grace of God. Eventually, he understood that, and he became even more determined to turn things around and make the most of his life.

But that didn't mean he didn't still struggle. Sometimes more than others. He was still human; he still needed God's strength and correction in his life. The truth was, what he'd come to understand was that it wasn't his own strength and abilities that determined his life. Before the accident, he always thought things were going well for him because of what he did. That's why the pressure had become too much; he thought that if he failed in any way, the whole thing might come crashing down around him. But really, it was God alone who sustained him. It is by His will that all have their existence. That's why the things his father said that night after pizza had struck a nerve. He'd done exactly the opposite of what he had planned—at the first sign of weakness, he was trying to be Lisa's knight in shining armor. Sure, he'd told her the truth about his accident and how he found Jesus, but he was slipping back into old habits. He'd become overly concerned about how the revelation of his growing faith might impact their friendship. He was trying to take control from God. He'd forgotten that surrender had to be a daily practice.

Scott sniffed, holding back tears. He'd done his best lately to keep his emotions under control. But it was a struggle; it seemed like every day he was either fighting depression or battling extreme bouts of anger, often unsuccessfully. He had shed many tears over recent months. Tears that were often a result of the realization of everything he'd put his family through, even before the accident. Many nights, he'd broken curfew to stay out drinking with friends, or argued with his parents just to get his way. Still, they'd continued to love and pray for him.

I'm sorry, Lord. In all the chaos, I've forgotten. I am a work in progress and need to be reminded of your presence in my life. Yes, you've given me an amazing opportunity to witness to Lisa. Still, somewhere along the way, I let it turn into something else. Please forgive me; let her see past my human failures and see You. That's the only way this is going to work. Amen.

Lisa flopped on her bed and flipped open her laptop. As much as she disliked Scott at the moment, his message was reaching her. But it didn't explain Gabe's message or what she could expect of God.

Over an hour passed as she did a web search of terms like "angels" and "messages from angels," but especially "Gabriel." She favored several websites on her browser that referred to him as the "Christmas Angel," referenced in the first chapter of the Gospel of Luke. Deciding to dig even deeper, she opened the Bible Scott gave her and found the book of Luke. She skimmed the first chapter. It told the story of how Gabriel appeared to Mary, telling her she would conceive a child as a virgin, a boy she was to name Jesus, and that this child would be king of a kingdom with no end. He also spread the hope of a child to a relative of hers, Elizabeth, who had been barren and was beyond her childbearing years, and her husband

Zachariah. The baby, Gabriel said, was to be called "John." John, the angel said, would lead many back to the faith they once held dear.

How strange it was that Jesus would come to earth to save His people in the form of a baby when He could have come as He was and done the same thing.

Yes. I could've done things that way, Lisa, but that would've been the easy route. I wanted to experience life from your point of view. How could I understand your pain if I never walked as one of you. That was part of my Father's plan.

The voice had come from nowhere, but she wasn't scared.

"What plan?" she said.

Scanning further in the chapters, she found a verse that made her heart skip a beat. It said: *Ask and it will be given to you; seek and you will find; knock and the door will be opened. For everyone who asks receives; the one who seeks finds; and to the one who knocks, the door will be opened.* Although the passage didn't directly answer her question, it sparked her interest in learning more about Jesus and His plan to save his people. More importantly, how it impacted her now, so many years later.

This must be another sign.

Yes, my daughter. You are on a difficult road. I understand. Keep going, and don't give up. I will never give up on you.

The soft reassurance whispered in her soul as her eyes grew tired. She placed the Bible next to her on the bed and closed her eyes.

Finally, she was beginning to believe.

"What are you smiling about?" Lisa asked, looking up from her reading.

"I'm just happy, that's all," Aunt Jane said, her eyes glistening. "Your uncle would be too, if he were here."

"There's one thing I still don't quite understand; why have the Ten Commandments if Jesus didn't intend for His followers to use them?"

"That's a toughie, especially for someone just starting in the faith. But here's the short version: Before Jesus' final act of sacrifice on the cross, many believed they had to follow these strict rules to get into heaven. It was inevitable they would fall into sin. When they did, they had to present a perfect and spotless animal to the priests as a living sacrifice for their sin—that was part of their first Covenant with God. When Christ died, however, animal sacrifices were no longer needed. Christ served as the ultimate sacrifice, for any sins committed in the past and present. Now, the Ten Commandments testify that we all need a Savior. We are all human, prone to fall short, both in word and deed."

"That explains much about grace and God's redemption plan after the Fall, but why did God choose to give us free will? I mean, He saw the consequences of Adam and Eve's choice. Why didn't he just stop them from eating the fruit of the forbidden tree ?"

"A lot of people have tried to answer that question through different doctrines, like predestination and free will. I believe God loves us so much, He gave us the power to make our own choices. Jesus wants to have a real, authentic relationship with us based on mutual love and respect."

CHAPTER 18

This was ridiculous—absolutely ridiculous!

Scott fumed as he sat in his bedroom looking through career brochures his mother had picked up at his physical therapy appointment. Jobs that didn't require the use of one's legs. Computer technology, research assistant . . . not exactly his strengths. All his talents were related to his physical abilities.

It had been almost two weeks since his last heart-to-heart with his father, and still no word from Lisa. That was okay. She just needed time; at least, that's what he kept telling himself. Over the last two weeks, he'd made a real effort in investing his time and energy with his family and giving Lisa space. Most importantly, he had tried to refocus on God.

Spending time with his family was even more important to him now. They had done so much for him in the last year; he had much to make up for. His behavior hadn't just made his parents' lives difficult but also his brothers'. Because of him, they had experienced a lack of stability and harmony at home. His parents' disagreements over how to manage Scott's behavior had been unsettling for them. However, the accident was even more traumatic as they watched him lie unconscious in the hospital bed. Scott had been their hero. Invincible.

Scott frowned. He hated thinking this way, but it was true. His brothers didn't look up to him like before. Who could blame them? He'd let everyone down.

He'd had to relearn even the most basic tasks; it took weeks for him to learn how to maneuver himself from his bed to the wheelchair, and he still struggled with many of the daily routines, like dressing or pulling his own pants up. It had also taken time to mentally adjust to his limitations, and those weeks and months had not been without fits of anger, expressed through throwing things, swearing, and tears.

Father, forgive my selfishness over the past year. I'm sorry it took an accident for you to get my attention. But now you've got it. I'm yours to use wherever you see fit. I'm glad you've seen fit to give me a second chance with my friend, Lisa. But don't let my affection for her block any other opportunities that may cross my path. Allow the rest of this summer to be a restoration for my family and me; I've already missed out on so much. Amen.

Scott blinked back tears. Until recently, he hadn't really considered the impact his accident had on his family. He'd been too busy trying to put his own life back together. Now God was beginning to help him understand the consequences of his choices and the need for healing in his family. But instead of relying on his faith to get their family through the tough times, far too often he relied on himself. That was an area where he still needed work.

What kind of example had he been to Devon and Marcel? Would they end up following in his footsteps? He certainly hoped not. As exciting as his popularity looked from the outside, it had never been enough. He always needed more—more wins, more sponsorships, more praise—but none of it ever filled the emptiness he felt inside. The excitement always faded, and the sport always demanded more.

It was after his accident that he finally realized none of those things mattered in the long term, and they could be taken away in an instant. Scott began devoting his time to rekindling his faith and focusing on things of eternal value. Sure, he still loved basketball and always would, but now that he'd probably never play again, the pressure of winning was gone. He could get back to loving the game! He would teach his brothers to love the game again and, more importantly, teach them the importance of faith and commitment to God.

But despite his improvement at keeping his focus on God and his family, he still couldn't get Lisa completely off his mind. He still felt he needed to connect with her. He decided he would call Lisa's aunt. If she refused to talk with him, fine; at least he'd be able to speak with Aunt Jane and make sure they were doing okay. If she happened to share more about her niece's activities over the past few weeks, even better.

"Two weeks, Lord . . . isn't that giving her space?"

"Who are you talking to?" A voice said from behind him.

Scott jumped and swung around to find Marcel standing in the doorway.

"None of your beeswax, mister. What have I told you about sneaking up on me?"

"That it's bad and I shouldn't do it."

"Exactly . . . yet here you are!"

"I'm sorry."

"Sorry doesn't cut it. Next time, I'm telling Mom and letting her deal with you. You know what that means."

Marcel frowned and began slowly backing out of the doorway.

Ugh. He'd done it again.

"Wait, Marcel."

Marcel stopped.

"I'm sorry, buddy. I shouldn't have reacted like that; I'm a little distracted right now. I know things have been tough for you and Devon. I'd love to make it up to you, just as soon as I'm done here. Deal?"

Marcel's face lit up, and he nodded vigorously.

"Now, run along and play. Before you know it, I'll be done, and I'll beat you both at a game of Uno."

Marcel's smile stretched even farther across his face, then he turned and raced away.

There. That's better.

Before he could stop himself, Scott pulled open the left pocket on his wheelchair in search of his cell phone. He pulled it out, and, without hesitation, found the number and pressed "Call."

"Hello?"

"Hi, Mrs. Mitchell, it's Scott. Scott McCarthy."

"Hello, dear. It's so nice to hear from you," Jane said cheerfully.

"I'm sorry to bother you, but . . . well, Lisa hasn't called me since our last visit, and I know she's mad, but . . . well . . . I'm sorry, I don't mean to put you in an awkward situation. I just wanted to check on her. How's our girl doing?"

Scott smacked his forehead. *How's our girl doing?* What was he thinking? Silence followed.

Had she hung up?

Just as he was about to press "End" and dial again, Mrs. Mitchell's voice broke through the silence.

"Sorry, Scott. I had to leave the room. I didn't want Lisa to know I was talking to you. I'm so glad you called, though. We're doing wonderful, actually. But you're right; Lisa's not too happy with you right now."

He'd already known it was true, but hearing it confirmed still hit him hard.

"I understand. But she's all right?"

"Yes. In fact, even better than all right." She chuckled. "I know Lisa says she's upset with you, but that's not my business. But whatever you said to her must have struck a chord. Over the last few weeks, her whole perspective on God has changed."

"How so?"

"Well, for starters, she's reading the Bible you gave her. I can't tell you how many times I tried to talk to her about God before, and she just shut down. Now, though, she's asking me questions all the time. It's pretty amazing."

"Wow! I wish I could see that for myself."

"Well, maybe you and Lisa can mend things. I'm sure she really wants to."

"I'm not sure about that. We left things on pretty bad terms."

Scott took a breath, then divulged the details of his visit, his confession about the accident, and his attempt to share his faith.

"It's not like I meant to lie to her, it's just that I wasn't comfortable admitting what I had done. It was hard enough admitting it to myself."

"I see." Jane said.

"I'm so sorry, Mrs. Mitchell. Like I said, I don't mean to put you in the middle of all this. I know I've disappointed everyone. I'm just so sorry."

"Scott, stop. It's not for me to judge, but . . ."

Scott let out a breath. *Here it comes.*

". . . I'm sure you've been forgiven by everyone concerned, but I think there might be someone more important whose forgiveness you need to seek."

"I know, I know. But I don't know if Lisa will ever truly forgive me."

"No, Scott, that's not who I mean. You need to forgive yourself. It sounds to me like you still haven't forgiven yourself for that night."

"Uhh . . . myself?" Scott said, running his hand down his paralyzed leg, subconsciously acknowledging the evidence of his bad choices. Could Mrs. Mitchell be right? As much as he tried, it was true—he couldn't stop replaying the day of his accident over and over in his mind, and the guilt always returned. If only he hadn't gotten drunk that night.

"You still there, Scott?"

"Yes, ma'am, I'm still here. Just thinking."

"You're still carrying that guilt, aren't you? You may be able to hide it from everyone, but you can't hide it from yourself or from God. I understand the weight of guilt. After Frank died, I spent a lot of time rewinding the events of that day, hour by hour. Sometimes minute by minute. What if I had done something differently? What if he hadn't been alone in the barn? As if something I could have done would have changed the outcome."

She was quiet for a moment. Scott waited for her to continue.

"It affected everything in my life. I was stuck there, on that day. It wasn't until someone at church came along and asked me an unusual question that I began to see things in a whole different light."

Scott leaned back in his wheelchair, intrigued. "What did he ask?"

"He said, 'Why do you think Jesus died on the cross for you?'"

Confused, Scott waited again for her to continue.

She chuckled. "I confess I didn't think that had anything to do with what I was feeling. I answered him in the typical way, explaining that Jesus loves me so much He died on the cross to cleanse me of all my sins."

"What's wrong with that?"

"Nothing. Mike just pointed out that Jesus' act on the cross is much more than that."

"What do you mean?"

"It's not just about our sins, Scott. We're His sons and daughters, and He wants a relationship with us. Don't you see? He doesn't want us living in the past. He wants us to look toward our future, both here on earth as well as in heaven. He wants us to live life without regret. After all, Jesus told us Himself in John 10:10, 'I have come that they may have life and have it to the full.'"

Scott had never thought of it that way. But it made sense.

"Thanks, I'm going to keep that in mind," he said. "And thanks for the talk. I'm glad things are going well. I guess I'll wait until Lisa contacts me. I'll leave it up to you whether you mention I called. You know what's best."

"Okay, dear. I'll be keeping you both in my prayers. Sounds like you two can use it."

"Thanks, I really appreciate it."

"Lisa, move your books off the table; dinner will be ready soon," Aunt Jane said, stirring the pot of pasta. "It's been hours, and I'm sure your eyes could use a break."

"But, Aunt Jane, I really should . . ." Lisa stretched and did her best to stifle a yawn. As much as she hated admitting it, her aunt was right. For two weeks, she'd been going at it, reading all she could about Jesus and His ministry. After all that, she had more questions than answers.

"I don't want to hear another word about it. Even Jesus had to eat and spend time with friends."

"Okay, you don't have to say anything more. I'm cleaning my stuff up as we speak."

Picking up her books from the table, Lisa watched her aunt quizzically. She'd seemed slightly off since the phone call she'd walked out of the room to take earlier. Had Mike called? What if he pressured her to change her mind about his proposal? She hoped that wasn't it!

She still wasn't sure about Mike, but she'd never seen Aunt Jane light up the way she did around him. He really seemed to make her happy. Of course, their relationship was nothing like hers and Uncle Frank's; that kind of love could only grow from years of commitment and testing. Still, Aunt Jane deserved to be happy again, and it was what Uncle Frank would've wanted. Plus, Mike had made it very clear he didn't intend to replace her uncle; instead, he honored his memory by coming alongside Jane in her grief.

That's what Christians were supposed to do, right?

At least, that's what she'd read.

"You seem a bit off this evening. Everything all right?" Lisa asked.

"Me? Oh yes, dear, I'm fine. I was just thinking about the McCarthys."

What had spurred her to think about them? Now of all times?

"Wait a minute . . ." Lisa eyed her aunt. "Did you talk to Scott?"

Aunt Jane continued in silence, stirring the pot.

"That little ..."

"Stop it." Aunt Jane spun around from the stove and stared straight into Lisa's eyes. "It's one thing for you to be mad at him, but it's another thing entirely for you to start calling him names. Are you really so willing to throw away his friendship?"

"So it *was* Scott on the phone! Well, I guess I know whose side you're on." Lisa folded her arms over her chest.

"It's not about sides, Lisa. The boy obviously cares about you. The fact that he's opened up the most personal, intimate details of his life with you should tell you that."

"*Ooooh*, intimate details." Lisa raised a brow, teasingly.

"Lisa! That's not what I mean, and you know it."

"Sorry." She unfolded her arms and placed her hands in her lap.

"I'm serious, Lisa. Scott has turned his life around, and he's sharing very personal issues with you. He's learned valuable lessons from his mistakes, and you might learn a thing or two from him. I can't help but think this is an act of redemption for him as well."

"Act of redemption? What's that supposed to mean?"

"Lisa, Scott knows he made a mistake. He knows he handled telling you the truth badly. He's seeking forgiveness. I can tell without a doubt that he still blames himself for his accident and the long-term impact it may have on his family. You should give the boy another chance. You know you're not the only one hurting." Aunt Jane aimed her wooden spoon at Lisa pointedly. "And he's not the only one who's made mistakes in their relationships either."

"Fine. I'll think about it. Under one condition."

Aunt Jane grabbed a pair of oven mitts from the drawer. "And that is?"

"You need to call Mike and resolve things with him. I'm still not comfortable with an engagement, but it's obvious he cares about you, and you care about him. Who am I to stand in the way of that? I really mean it this time. I've been selfish. From what I've read in the Bible, real love isn't selfish. I'm so sorry if I hurt you. You deserve to be happy. Turns out I really do still have a lot to learn."

As she spoke, emotions built inside of her. She hadn't expected to feel this way, but suddenly she burst into tears and rushed into her aunt's embrace. "I'm so sorry, Aunt Jane. I'm so sorry for not loving you how I should have."

"Oh, honey," Aunt Jane said, holding her tightly and kissing her forehead. "I love you, and I'll take you just the way you are."

Lisa had spent much of the last year trying to prove herself worthy of her parents' love and affection, but now she understood the true meaning of love. Love was unconditional. She didn't have to earn it; it was just there, steady, and constantly waiting for her with open arms.

Aunt Jane had helped her to understand that.

After a long embrace, Lisa stepped away from Aunt Jane and swiped a hand across her face to wipe away the tears. "I'd better wash my face before dinner; I must look awful." She hurried toward the bathroom.

Glancing at herself in the mirror, Lisa had to admit her emotions had been running high lately. What was wrong with her? She'd cried more tears in the past weeks than she remembered crying at her own brother's funeral.

Why had God chosen now, this summer, to reach her? Why hadn't He shown Himself to her earlier?

"I need to stop this," she said. She couldn't keep doing this; it wasn't healthy. If she'd learned anything this summer, it was that living in the past wasn't helpful; nor did it change anything. It was time for a new beginning.

This trip had helped her change and grow in ways she could never have imagined. First, by forcing her to come to grips with her own grief over the loss of her brother and the sudden death of her uncle. Second, she'd reconnected with Scott, and, in doing so, he'd helped her unlock a part of herself she didn't know was even there.

It's because you are starting to recognize me, daughter . . . Don't stop! Keep searching, and you will find me, I promise. Seek me with all your heart.

She stared at the mirror and recalled the passage from the prophet Jeremiah that she read in the Old Testament, a gentle pleading to the people of Israel.

"For I know the plans I have for you," declares the Lord, "plans to prosper you and not to harm you, plans to give you hope and a future. Then you will call on me and come and pray to me, and I will listen to you. You will seek me and find me when you seek me with all your heart. I will be found by you."

Was God speaking to her like that? How wonderful it would be if He were!

CHAPTER 19

Glancing at the clock, Lisa grimaced; two a.m. Where had the time gone? After eating dinner with Aunt Jane, she'd made a promise that she'd go to bed at a decent hour. So much for that.

Letting out a deep breath, she leaned back in her chair and surveyed the materials spread out on the kitchen table before her. Over the last two weeks, Lisa had read more books than she had during her entire school year. If only she'd picked up the habit of studying like this a bit sooner, maybe she wouldn't have flunked her classes or faced the threat of not graduating with her classmates.

But that would've meant never going to Aunt Jane's, missing out on the opportunity to reconnect with her and Scott, and missing the opportunity for spiritual and emotional growth. She was coming to understand and accept herself in a whole new light, and that was due entirely to her being here at Aunt Jane's. Granted, it hadn't worked out exactly as planned; instead of finding an escape at Aunt Jane's, she'd found new challenges.

Warmth crept slowly up her neck onto her cheeks as she remembered her reaction to finding Aunt Jane in the arms of a strange man. She had to admit, they acted in love; they seemed to enjoy spending time together and shared similar interests. Even more evident was the fact that they had developed a deep emotional commitment to each other based on their shared faith in Jesus and their commitment to their church.

That is, until a couple of weeks ago …

Shaking her head, Lisa pushed her chair away from the table, then closed all the books and set them in a pile. Poor Mike. No doubt about it, he'd gotten the raw end of the deal; not only had he lost the love of his life, but his integrity had been questioned. Guilt weighed on Lisa like a heavy blanket. Thinking back to her actions toward Mike and their conversations, she realized he'd been nothing but nice to her, even trying to relate to her on a personal level by sharing his own family's story. Throughout his relationship with Aunt Jane, he had kept his word and stayed by her side, loving her, but allowing her the time she needed to grieve for Uncle Frank. He had put her needs and heart before his own, even when that meant staying away. In return for all he'd done, Lisa had managed to alienate him and treat him like an intruder.

How's that even possible? To love someone so much that you are willing to let them go?

Only through me, my daughter . . . Haven't you learned that by now?

Chuckling, Lisa walked up the stairs and into her bedroom. Growing more familiar by the day, the still, small voice certainly made sense. Not only had she read about God's love in Scripture, she'd experienced it firsthand in Aunt Jane's love and acceptance, as well as in Scott's absolute honesty.

So now what?

Slipping into her pajamas and hopping into bed, Lisa hoped her aunt would take their conversation to heart and give Mike another chance. She clicked off the lamp beside the bed and laid back into the pillows. Mike was a good guy. Not only did he care for her, but also he had proven he could put up with all of her antics!

Smiling, Lisa closed her eyes. Who else had done that for her?

Oh, but I can too, my daughter. If only you'd believe.

Bolting upright, Lisa glanced around the room. She was alone, but the voice had spoken as clear as day. Settling down in the bed again, she closed her eyes and drifted off to sleep.

Despite staying up late the night before, Lisa woke refreshed on Sunday morning, ready to make some changes in her life. Maybe going to church wasn't such a bad idea after all; it'd probably help make sense of what she'd read so far in the Bible and clarify what this voice was trying to tell her.

"Mind if I tag along this Sunday?"

Startled, Aunt Jane turned to see Lisa, standing in her bedroom door and wearing a floral blouse and a plain black skirt.

"Oh, honey, nothing would make me happier." She hurried across the room and hugged Lisa.

"Thank you," Aunt Jane whispered.

"What was that?" Lisa asked, stepping out of Aunt Jane's arms.

"Oh, nothing, just talking to myself." Aunt Jane took one last look in the mirror, and then picked up her purse. "I think I'm ready. How about you?"

"I think so. Is what I'm wearing okay?" Lisa said. "It's all I could match from the pieces in my suitcase."

"Sweetheart, you look perfect, and anyway, the people at this church aren't concerned with how you dress. God isn't either. This world is full of hurting people looking for answers. He's more concerned about the state of people's hearts."

"You mean people like me?"

"Especially people like you. Jesus' invitation is open to everyone. We are all hurting in one way or another—it's just that some scars are more visible than others."

"Like Scott's disability, you mean."

"Exactly. But we can talk more about that later; if I keep answering your questions, we're gonna be late for church."

"Oh, sorry."

Aunt Jane chuckled. "I'm just kidding, honey. They always have at least fifteen minutes of music and fellowship, followed by worship. I just don't want you to miss the music. God always manages to speak to me through the songs. I hope He does the same for you."

"God speaks to you, then?"

"Yes, although not always in the literal sense. Why do you ask?"

"Nothing really, it's just something you said sounded vaguely familiar to something my good friend Melissa told me before coming here for this summer."

"Oh?"

"Yeah, Melissa said God speaks to her through her daily Bible readings."

"You have a pretty smart friend there; I'd keep her if I were you. We'd better go before all the good spots are taken."

"Seriously? Is your church that popular?"

"No, honey. I'm just kidding again. But we need to get going; I didn't have enough time to make coffee this morning, but if we're lucky, they'll still be serving some in the foyer at church."

Aunt Jane followed Lisa out of the room and into the hallway. She pulled her close. "Come on, let's go. I can't wait to show you off."

"Show me off? Like a pony?"

"Yes!" Aunt Jane said. "You'll be my pretty little pony today!"

They both burst into laughter as they stepped out of the house and toward the car. Fifteen minutes later, they pulled into a middle school parking lot.

"Wait, I thought the church was back there?" Lisa asked, pointing to the road behind them.

"It is, but it's under construction right now. The deacons felt that in order for us to grow and increase our outreach, we needed to make some changes to the building. That's why we're adding wheelchair ramps, an outdoor playground for the children, and a gaming area built specifically for the teens. The plans are amazing. They should be completed some-time next year. Until then, we meet here for church."

"Oh, wow."

"Come on. It's not as bad as it looks; at least you're not going to be tested on what you learn today." Aunt Jane winked, grabbed her niece's hand, and pulled her toward the entrance.

Lisa cringed. Though the landscape remained manicured, the one-story building clearly needed work—its red brick, once bright with color and promise, was now a faded orange, aged by time and sunlight.

"Come on, it'll be fine."

Nodding, she followed her aunt into the building. She'd never imag-ined setting foot in any school again, at least not until she'd had children of her own and enough distance from her own school days that she could look back on her youth and smile. But here she was, about to face memories of her school years head on again.

Hello, welcome to New Life Church." A middle-aged man greeted them with a smile and slipped in front of them to hold open the door. "You just made it; service is about to start."

"Thank you, Charlie." Aunt Jane slipped inside then motioned toward Lisa, coming in behind her. "This is my niece, Lisa. She's visiting me this summer and decided to tag along today."

"Lisa, so nice to finally meet you. Your aunt talks about you often. Now I have a face to put to the name."

Lisa smiled politely, lifting her eyes to meet Charlie's, and nodded shyly. After all, what could she say to a stranger after just meeting him?

Sunlight streamed through the doors. It took a few moments for Lisa's vision to adjust to the lighting inside. When she did, her eyes focused on the long hallway lined with silver lockers. As a first-year high school student, she'd expected the next four years of her education to be full of adventure and excitement. Boy was she wrong! As freshman, still sporting pigtails and tie-dyed clothing, Lisa quickly became the target of bullying from other students. A rush of memories flooded her mind. The gray walls of the school building slowly began closing in on her, making it difficult to breathe. Her mouth went dry.

Please don't have an anxiety attack here—especially in front of these strangers! Please, not here, not now. Calm down, Lisa. Breathe and count . . .1, 2, 3 . . . and exhale . . . 1, 2, 3 . . .

The exercise did its job quickly, slowing her racing heart to a steadier pace, though her palms were slightly damp, no one seemed to notice her panic as the three of them worked their way down the hallway toward the sound of music.

Charlie, again, held the door for them and inside motioned toward three empty seats near the back of the room. Aunt Jane quietly nodded in agreement and worked toward the middle of the aisle. Lisa followed quietly behind her, and then Charlie, who took the aisle seat. Looking around, she couldn't help but notice how happy everyone seemed to be there.

"Good morning, everyone." A man with silver-gray hair spoke from behind a wooden pulpit at the front of the room. "Welcome to New Life Church. Will you join me in singing hymn number 222?"

As the first song concluded, a young man, in Bermuda shorts, and untucked shirt, went to the front and introduced himself as Todd, the church's youth pastor. He invited the congregation to join him in the opening prayer.

"Dear Lord, we come to you today with open hearts and minds. Amid the busyness of life, may we never forget that you guide our every step. May you bless Pastor Brad as he speaks to our graduating seniors who are embarking on a new chapter. As they approach the most exciting and challenging time of their adult lives, protect them as their faith is tested, and help them to share their faith with others. May we each reflect on our own journeys of faith as Pastor shares the word with us. In Jesus' name we pray. Amen."

Todd returned to his seat. Before he could sit, though, an elderly woman with short silver hair gestured for the congregation to stand and join her in song.

Great, just great.

What miserable timing she had. The one time she invited herself to church, the sermon was directed toward graduation, and the wonderful futures the students had ahead of them. Had the entire world turned against her? Could she not just once catch a break?

Pushing the thought from her mind, she allowed herself to be immersed in the music. Each beautiful melody soothed her soul in ways she never imagined. One song in particular talked about the many different attributes of God and how He could be trusted. The chorus was beautiful and easy to sing, but she still struggled with what worshipping God really meant, especially with everything in her life falling apart.

There was Scott. There was her family. Some things seemed beyond repair, beyond turning around. But she felt hopeful for the first time in a very long time. The scriptures she had read and the things her aunt had shared had given her that.

Okay, God, you got my attention. I've done all I can on my own. If you're real, show me.

Shooting the prayer heavenward, Lisa wondered how He would answer. After all, this sermon was meant for graduating seniors, not for her.

"Thank you, Todd, for that wonderful prayer and introduction to today's sermon," an older man with graying hair said, taking his place behind the podium. "My name's Brad Owens, and as Todd said, I'm the senior pastor here at New Life Church. I'd like to welcome any visitors we may have today; we're so happy you've chosen to join us. Since it's summer, we've decided to forgo our regular sermon series in favor of a somewhat timely topic. Many of our parishioners are on vacation, which got me thinking . . . with most of our seniors graduating and many heading off to college, this will probably be one of the last sermons they hear from me in this place, so I'd better make it a good one."

Laughter filled the room.

"In all seriousness, though, Todd's right. Going away to college is one of the most exciting times in a young person's life, meeting new people, and experiencing things on your own for the very first time. Believe it or not, I felt the same way growing up. As the eldest of three siblings, I was responsible for ensuring we all got home safely after school, since my parents worked during the day. You see, my mother worked as a cashier while my dad helped to unload shipments at the local warehouse, so, you can imagine my parents' shock when I told them one day that I planned to go away to college. Don't get me wrong, they were proud, because I was the first in our family to consider getting a degree. But they were concerned about how they were going to cover all the expenses. It didn't matter because, by the end of the school year, I had earned a four-year scholarship to the Moody Bible Institute in Chicago, hoping to someday become a pastor. And here I am." He held out his hands and smiled.

Lisa scoffed inwardly. *Yes, and I'm sure they're still bragging about it, even in their old age. "Oh, yes, Brad was the first one in our family to ever get a degree. And look at him now . . . pastor of his very own church in Ohio. Blah, blah, blah. Can you please get to the point, pastor?"*

Aunt Jane glanced in her direction as if sensing her discomfort.

"I'm so sorry," she mouthed.

Lisa rolled her eyes playfully and shoved her gently on the arm.

Slinking down in her seat, she continued to listen to the sermon.

" . . . The week of my orientation finally came, and there we were, crammed like sardines, with all my personal belongings in my family's 1985 coupe, bound for Chicago. By the end of the trip, I couldn't wait to get out of there and have a place on my own . . . "

Great, just what I wanted to hear. The pastor's perfect journey of faith and countless adventures with lifelong friends. Just once, can't someone be honest and talk about the issues teenagers face daily?

"Imagine my surprise when I realized I would be sharing a small bathroom with three other guys—just like I had back home. I guess what I'm trying to say is this: as much as I'd like to paint a happy picture of my college experience, I'm not going to do that. Parts of it were happy, yes, but for the most part, I felt challenged and stretched beyond my wildest dreams—even to the point where I felt like going home. Now, everyone's experience will be different, and I can't guarantee what happened to me won't happen to you—I hope it doesn't, but you will undoubtedly be academically and spiritually challenged. It might be as simple as solving a disagreement with your roommate or standing up for your faith in front of your classmates and professor. Either way, I want you to be as prepared as possible to deal with whatever may come your way. That's why I've entitled today's sermon: Dear Younger Me: Learning to Stand on the Foundation of Your Faith, the Bible."

"Now, I don't want you to get the wrong idea. Yes, this message was written specifically for seniors going off to college, but it is meant for everyone—from the person who believes in Jesus to their very core, but current circumstances have caused them to doubt His sincerity, all the way to the complete skeptic."

Now we're getting somewhere. Granted, I wouldn't call myself a complete skeptic after everything I've been through. But somewhere in the middle.

"You see, it's essential that we, as believers, never forget where the foundation of our faith comes from. We are all created in God's image with the express purpose of having a relationship with Him. That all changed instantly when Eve chose to listen to the serpent and she and Adam ate from the forbidden fruit on the tree in the center of the Garden. Because of man's moment of weakness, Jesus had to play the role of intercessor for us, coming down to earth as a baby and growing up to experience all the trials and tribulations of being a human."

"Unlike us, though, He didn't sin and became the perfect and spotless sacrifice necessary to restore our relationship with God. As Romans 3:23 says, 'For all have sinned and fall short of the glory of God.' We are sinners in need of redemption. We need to be rescued, or saved, from our hopeless situation."

Me, a sinner? I don't know if I would go that far. I know I'm not perfect, but I guess, if I'm being honest with myself . . . yes, I've sinned. I don't steal, and I haven't killed anyone, but I'm a sinner, nonetheless.

"I bet you're saying to yourself, 'Gee thanks, pastor, for reminding me of my past. But that's just it; remembering your past is the key to truly embracing and accepting God's gift of eternal life. Yes, we've sinned, but in the Father's infinite mercy, He doesn't leave us alone to clean up our own mess. In fact, He does the complete opposite—sending His one and only Son to give up His life for our plight. All we need to do is believe and trust in Him. John reiterates this simple act of faith in the first chapter of his gospel, when he writes, 'As many as received Him, to them He gave the right to become children of God.' He continues explaining this subject of faith, saying in John 3:16–17, 'For God so loved the world that he gave his one and only Son, that whoever believes in him shall not perish but have eternal life. For God did not send his Son into the world to condemn the world, but to save the world through him.'

This all seems so technical. I understand the idea that Jesus died for us—for me. But is this the only way God could achieve His purpose? Why not just forgive everyone? Some people want nothing to do with God. So why not just forgive those who do?

Yes, I could do that, daughter, but you still wouldn't meet my standards.

So what do I do now?

"That's why we call this the gospel—it's the good news—because it tells the truth of God's love for us. He's done the hard part, paying the ultimate sacrifice for us on the cross. All that's left for us is to accept his free gift of salvation and believe in Jesus Christ as our Savior. This means repenting from our sin and allowing him to change from the inside out."

Pastor Brad went on to explain that the disciple John valued the act of believing so much that he mentioned the topic almost one hundred times in his gospel, even going as far as saying that he hoped it served as an eyewitness account so that those who heard it might believe.

"Now I know believing in Jesus these days can be difficult; Jesus understands that too. After all, He experienced life's challenges just as you and I do. That's why He provided example after example of people in various stages of their faith—from the blind man Bartholomew, who was healed in Mark 10:51, to Martha, a grieving yet devoted follower of Christ after the death of her brother, Lazarus, in John 11. He posed the same question to each: 'What do you believe?' Though the answers ranged in variety from the blind man's quick response of 'Lord, I believe' to Martha's quiet affirmation of 'I believe you are the Messiah,' and even 'Lord, help me in my unbelief,' each person was given the same opportunity to make up their mind."

"In the end, Jesus rewarded them for their faith, no matter how small. I am saying this specifically to the person who may be hearing this message for the first time and wondering what's next? To you, I say, God sees you; He knows your heart and knows you've been searching for answers on your own, but that can only take you so far. Still, He understands the courage it took for you to come this far, and He will wait as long as He must for you to finally come to Him. Still, the Father is unbelievably happy to see you were able to join us today, as are we. Keep searching; I promise you will not come up empty."

CHAPTER 20

Pastor Brad stopped speaking, letting the full power of his words rest on the congregation. After a few moments of silence, his eyes moved across the congregation as if looking for something. Then his eyes met Lisa's, and he smiled. Instantly, she was covered in goosebumps. How in the world could he know? After all, until recently, she hadn't even considered the idea of a God, let alone entertained going to church. Now, here she was, listening in complete awe as a stranger spoke about the circumstances in her life. How was this possible? How was this happening?

My dear daughter, don't you see? Haven't I proven myself faithful throughout this trip?

Instantly, the faces of Scott, Aunt Jane, and Gabe flashed through her mind. Yes, she had to admit that they'd each played an integral part in getting her here today. Scott with his unique testimony of finding God through his paralysis, Aunt Jane with her unconditional love and encouragement. Then there was Gabe, whose mysterious appearance out of nowhere still mystified her. Though they'd just met, he seemed genuinely concerned about her. Why else would he stop what he was doing and come to her aid? In that one small act, it was as if he'd permitted her to release all her pent-up emotions and finally get real with God.

Yes, it had all led her here to this moment. And now she had the opportunity for a new life, one with God.

But what about Ryan? Where were you then?

Ryan would never get the chance to live his life. Never get the chance to become class president, go out for the football team, or get nominated prom king his senior year of high school. He hadn't deserved the leukemia that ended his life.

I don't get it, Lord. Why weren't you there then?

Oh, but I was, my dear. I've been here all along. Don't you remember Sherry, the volunteer candy striper, and the chaplain who stopped by during his lunch hour nearly every day? They were both my ambassadors.

Sherry was the young redheaded volunteer candy striper who had adopted Ryan as her "favorite patient." She had provided a welcome distraction for him from the string of doctors and nurses that filled his days. From the beginning, she'd seen Ryan differently than most of the staff; not as a kid with cancer, Sherry had seen him as just a kid. She'd helped keep his days as normal as possible, bringing classic board games and comic books whenever she could.

Ryan had looked forward to Sherry's visits; it was as if the sight of her smiling face brought him new life. Even as his chemo increased and his strength waned, he tried his best to stay awake during her visits. Sometimes, though, it wasn't enough.

"I guess today tired him out," Sherry said once, entering his room and sitting beside Lisa.

"Yeah. You just missed Mom. She's out talking to the doctors. It looks like the current dosage of chemo isn't working. Today they agreed to start him on something different. Poor little guy isn't handling it that well; he can't keep anything down and isn't quite himself." Lisa angled her body to gently rub her brother's hand. "He tried so hard, but he couldn't stay awake long enough to wait for you."

"Aww, poor guy. Well, I'll stop by in the morning before my shift to say hi." She turned to Lisa. "But how are you doing with all this, though?" She smiled warmly.

Stunned, Lisa sat silently for a moment. No one had ever asked her that question before. Conversations were always focused on Ryan and his cancer.

"Look, I know everything is tough right now. Your parents are occupied dealing with your brother, and I'm sure you feel left out. But you're not; I'm always here if you want to talk about anything—cancer-related or not."

From then on, Sherry and Lisa had been friends. Aside from her scheduled visits, she'd pop in more regularly when she knew Ryan would be asleep to chat. Lisa would never be able to thank her enough for those evening talks; they'd, brought comfort and encouragement.

Unfortunately, the two had lost touch after Ryan went into remission and left the hospital. Lisa had gone back to the hospital several times searching for her, but each time, nothing—apparently no one at the hospital knew who she was or remembered seeing her. When her brother relapsed just six months later, she'd searched the halls for Sherry every chance she had. She'd even asked administrators to check their employee records, but that search, too, revealed nothing.

It was as if Sherry had never existed.

Okay, you've got me there. But why here? Why now? I've still got so many questions that need to be answered.

Lisa turned her attention back to Pastor Brad as he resumed his message.

"Everyone thinks that as Christians, we have all the answers. I'll be the first to tell you I don't, but I trust the One who does. Granted, the answers may not always look the way we would imagine. We must always remember, we live in an imperfect world tainted by sin. But God promises to make things right if we only believe in Him."

Okay, let's say for the moment that I believe. What now?

"True belief is not for the faint of heart. It takes a lot of faith. Remember that even the Evil One acknowledges Jesus' identity, but trusting in Him is entirely different. It involves acknowledging your weaknesses, laying them down at the feet of Jesus, and allowing Him to change you. For some, this may come easy, for others, not so much. It can be scary stepping out into the unknown and relinquishing control over to God when you've learned to rely on yourself for so long. But when it's done, what a burden will be lifted from your soul! Now, just like any type of relationship, learning to rely on God takes time and a lot of commitment through reading your Bible and a consistent prayer life. But the gift of salvation is free and permanent. Once you've accepted Jesus as your Savior, you have been reconciled and adopted into his family; no longer do you walk this world alone. As it plainly states in Matthew 28:20, 'Surely, I am with you always to the very end of the age.' Yes, we still live in a sinful world, but this world is no longer our home. Our home is in heaven with the Lord Jesus Christ; one day, He is coming back for us. While we wait, we must remember, we do not live for ourselves and our desires. Instead, we live for Jesus. We have been given a new purpose to share God's love with those around us. That isn't to say we won't encounter obstacles along the way—we will. They will challenge our faith and tempt us to doubt; but by choosing to trust Him and walk in obedience, you will learn more about your Father and learn more about yourself in the process."

The pastor leaned on the podium and fell silent for a moment before continuing.

"Let's pray, shall we?"

Bowing her head, Lisa let the full weight of his message take root in her heart. She waited expectantly for his prayer to begin.

"Father, please let this sermon be an ever-present reminder of how important every child is in your eyes. You've created us for such amazing purposes, Lord; however, because of sin, we've strayed away from you. I will be forever thankful that you didn't leave us in such a lowly state. Instead, you set into action a plan of reconciliation for each and every one of us. All we need to do is ask. Please, let us ask ourselves whether we need to do that today. Let's not wait another moment. It's that important. I pray these things in your precious name. Amen."

As Pastor Brad invited the congregation to stand up for the final song, Lisa remained seated.

Okay, God, so I may have taken a little longer to see all the signs point-ing to you; for that, I am truly sorry. You and I know I can be stubborn sometimes; still, you never gave up on me. Thank you! Anyway, I'm here now and listening. Jesus, I'm tired of doing things alone; I know I need you, Lord. I realize now that I have strayed away from your purpose for my life and don't deserve your mercy. But because of your merciful act on the cross, I believe I am reconciled. I still have a lot to learn on this journey. Please be patient with me.

"Amen."

With that final word whispered aloud, Lisa stood to join the congregation in song.

True, she'd failed miserably trying to fix her family's problems, but that had all brought her here, to this moment and to this church. Standing amid all these people lifting their voices in praise of their Creator, she finally felt at peace. She was part of something bigger than herself, part of an eternal family, founded not on blood alone but on faith in Jesus Christ. And while she could do nothing to help her family at home, God could, and He would. She wiped away her tears, then grasped Aunt Jane's hand and sang the chorus one final time, lifting all her worries to her heavenly Father.

"What was that all about?" Aunt Jane whispered as they made their way out of the school's exit.

"What?" Lisa asked, smiling mischievously.

"You looked like you were praying in there, has something changed for you?"

"Maybe." Lisa laughed.

"Well, I want to know what it is."

"You mean that I finally believe Jesus loves me and died on the cross. Those aren't just words; I actually felt Him for the first time in my life, so much so that I asked him to be my Lord and Savior."

"Sweetheart, that's wonderful news; I know you've been struggling to make sense of the Bible and its impact on your life. I'm so happy for you."

"Granted, I still have a lot to learn . . ."

"Honey, if there's one thing I want you to remember from me today, it's this: Faith is a journey. Every day is a chance to learn something new about our Lord and Savior, Jesus Christ. Now come on, let's go celebrate your birthday, my treat."

Lisa giggled. "Aunt Jane, it's not my birthday!"

"It is now, sweetie. It's your spiritual birthday." She smiled then winked at Lisa. "I'll explain more on the way."

CHAPTER 21

Another week passed, and still no word from Lisa. Who could blame her? In one fell swoop, Scott had shattered any illusion of honesty they'd had. If only he had said something sooner, maybe she wouldn't have reacted so harshly.

"A little late now," Scott mumbled into his bowl of cereal. He had barely touched his breakfast; he was so distracted thinking about Lisa.

"What's that, son?" Mr. McCarthy asked, putting down his newspaper on the kitchen table. He shifted in his chair to face him.

"Oh, it's nothing, really. It's just that I haven't heard from Lisa or her aunt in a while, and I'm getting a little concerned, that's all."

His parents exchanged a knowing glance. At this point, both of them knew he was struggling with the situation.

"Son, Lisa will call you when she's ready," his father said. "You need to stop obsessing about it."

Scott knew his father was right, but he'd tried as hard as possible to get her off his mind and it hadn't worked. Yes, maybe he was obsessing. But it felt like he had no control over it.

"I know, I know. I just want to make sure everything's all right."

"Didn't you do that last week when you called and talked to her aunt?" his mother asked, a hint of mischief in her eyes.

He shrugged and shot a glance over at his dad. Of course he had shared their previous conversation with his mom. Why wouldn't he? They weren't the type of couple to keep secrets from one another; the only question on Scott's mind was how much he had shared.

"I did. She was fine. Her aunt said she'd been reading the Bible for the past few weeks, and I'd just like to know if any of it's sinking in. I'd really like to hear it from Lisa."

"Yes, I'm sure you would, Scott," his mom said, picking up her coffee mug and taking it to the sink, "but like we discussed earlier, these things take time. I'm sure she's still reeling from your last conversation. You'd be crazy to add anything on top of that."

"I agree with your mother, son. Like I told you, you've done your part; you've shared your faith with Lisa, and we're proud of you for that. Now it's time for you to let go and let God take charge. Remember what I said about playing hero. You need to stay out of the way, so the Holy Spirit has room to move in Lisa's heart."

"And," his mother said softly, turning to look directly at him, "you need to put your personal feelings for Lisa aside before things get too complicated."

Scott knew this was coming. He'd heard the same thing from his father only days before. As much as he appreciated their advice and concerns, it drove him nuts that they still didn't fully trust his judgment.

His mother continued. "We're not saying we would disapprove of a relationship between the two of you in the future. We're just suggesting you wait. Both of you need time to work through your own personal struggles. Your faith is growing, and you're on the path to accepting things as they are now; but we know you're still struggling to reconcile your life in a wheelchair."

"Lisa is just now starting her journey, too," his father said, "taking her first steps toward a relationship with Christ and understanding what it means to have faith."

His mother sat back at the table. "She's got to recognize her need for Jesus is greater than anything else. Even you."

Scott rolled his eyes. "Geez, Mom."

She shook her head. "If Lisa becomes a Christian, and we pray that she does, we don't want you two jumping into a relationship. She needs time to build her dependence on the Lord. If her family is falling apart at home like you said, she'll need that more than ever."

Scott huffed in surrender. You're right, Mom. I should wait for her to call me. It's just so hard not knowing how she is feeling about me—especially not knowing if she's still mad at me."

"That's just the thing, son. It's not about you," his father said.

Scott stared at his dad in shock. It was one thing to be called out when it was just the two of them, but—

"Don't look at me like that. We understand you're struggling with your emotions. Believe me, I remember being young and being in your shoes." He winked at Scott's mother. "We just don't want this attraction to interfere with your personal growth—spiritual or otherwise—and as difficult as it is for you to hear, we believe it already has."

His mom looked at him sympathetically. "You just haven't been yourself lately. At first, your intentions seemed honorable. But recently, your focus seems to have changed. You seem more focused on how Lisa feels about you."

"Really, Mom? Is that what you think of me?" Anger rushed through Scott as he jerked his wheelchair away from the table and headed for his room.

Scott flew into his room and slammed his bedroom door shut. He took a deep breath to calm himself.

He could hear his parents' faint voices as they continued to talk at the kitchen table. He already felt bad for the way he'd just stormed out in the middle of their conversation. Once again, he'd let his strong emotions control his actions.

He rolled to the door and listened to what they were saying. They were lifting him up in prayer. This made him feel even guiltier for the way he'd just reacted, but he couldn't deny that he needed it. There was still so much growth for him to do. Would he ever get to the place where he could display self-control, even when it was difficult? Sometimes it didn't feel like he would.

Scott picked up the basketball from the corner chair, tossing it back and forth between his hands.

Why did his parents have to be so right about everything? He'd done his best to remain focused on sharing his testimony, but it hadn't worked. Just being close to Lisa had totally derailed him. He'd been sulking around the house ever since, like a lovesick puppy. Daydreaming had become a habit, and he was losing sight of anything else.

"Dear Lord, what am I missing here? I'm really confused. I know I was called to witness to her, but now everything seems to be blowing up in my face. Please show me the way and help me do this right." Tears trickled down his cheek as he leaned back his head and closed his eyes. "Forgive me, Lord. The spirit is willing, but the flesh is weak."

"Don't you think it's about time you gave Scott a call, Lisa?" Aunt Jane said as they sat in the living room watching the singing competition "American Star." "I'm sure the boy is worried sick about you."

"And just how would you know that?" Lisa said, curled up in the over-stuffed chair across from her aunt. She tilted her head and smiled inquisitively. "You haven't been talking to Scott behind my back, have you?"

"And what if I have?" Aunt Jane said with a sly smile. "You've been avoiding him these past few weeks, and he's genuinely concerned he might have messed things up between you two. You didn't hear the desperation in his voice when he called last week; it was sweet, but quite pitiful."

Lisa turned her attention back to the television to avoid responding. Yes, Scott's concealment of his drinking and accident still stung. But she was beginning to see that she wasn't off the hook herself. Since her prayer and acceptance of Jesus, she had begun to recognize her own role in creating the situation between them. Although Scott's silence following his accident had hurt her deeply, she hadn't reached out to him either. What did that say about her? More importantly, what did that say about their friendship?

She was finally beginning to realize she had damaged their relationship as well, and blowing up at Scott hadn't made it better. He'd been sincere in apologizing and openly vulnerable, sharing his struggles and faith with her. It had to be difficult, and it must've taken courage.

And yet, I yelled at him and sent him away.

A slow flush crept up Lisa's neck and crept onto her cheeks as she let out a deep sigh of exasperation. So much for acting like an adult.

"Based on that reaction, I assume your feelings for him haven't changed." Aunt Jane said, teasing her.

"Haha. Very funny, Aunt Jane." She turned sideways in the chair and flipped her legs over the arm. "Of course, I still like him. I'm just not quite ready to see him again. I have a few things I need to figure out. Besides," she said, crossing her arms over her chest, "weren't you the one who warned me against having a relationship with him right now, so soon after becoming a Christian? I just want to make sure I'm on the right track with God before I see Scott again."

Aunt Jane chuckled. "And how long do you think that will take you? Lisa, maybe you're under the misconception that as a Christian, you will have things all figured out and everything in your life under control in no time. I assure you, you won't. Scott doesn't, and I certainly don't either. We're all just troubled people, taking it day by day and doing the best we can."

"But you seem to have everything figured out."

"Oh please," Aunt Jane said, flipping a hand in the air dismissively. "I'm far from having it all together. I think you'd know that by now. Fortunately, I have good friends and my church to help me along. New Life Church has been a true blessing to me. You'll need to find that sort of support when you get home too."

"And where do you suggest I find this support?"

"Well, you're welcome to join our women's Bible study while you're here. Of course, when you get back home, you'll want to find a strong Bible-teaching church near you. I'm sure Melissa will be more than happy to have you go with her, or maybe she can help you find one if that one isn't right for you."

Lisa hadn't thought about Melissa since she left home. She'd been so right about God working in her life this summer. Would she even believe the changes going on in her heart? Melissa had spoken courageously about her faith in the Lord and had planted the seed; now it was growing inside Lisa.

Lord, thank you for being so faithful to me amid my stubbornness. You were with me through it all, placing people in my path to encourage me along this journey to a new life. Especially Melissa. I realize now that I haven't been that great of a friend to her. Please help me change that. Amen.

Lifting her cell phone from the coffee table, Lisa found Melissa's contact and pressed, "Call."

"Finally taking my advice and calling Scott?"

"Wouldn't you like to know?" Winking, Lisa stood and pinned the phone between her ear and shoulder.

"Hey, watch who you're talking to, young lady," Aunt Jane said, tossing a pillow playfully in her niece's direction.

"I know, I know," Lisa laughed. "I'm gonna take this in my room."

"Okay, but don't make it too long. You promised you'd get back to your studies if I let you watch some television. You still have a lot of work to finish, young lady."

"I know, I know," she called out over her shoulder as she climbed the stairs to her room.

CHAPTER 22

"Hey, girlfriend!" Melissa's voice practically purred through the phone.

"Hey, friend. How are things back home?"

"Pretty good. I've already started packing for the family cruise, although my mom says if I pack any more I'll pay the airport overweight fees on my own." Melissa laughed. "You should see my room; it's a disaster. There are clothes everywhere and barely enough room for me to sit. But enough about me; how are you? How is your summer going at your aunt's?"

"Yeah, well, that's why I'm calling you actually. I need to ask you for a favor."

"Okay, you know I'm here for you; whatever you need, just ask."

As always, her friend had clearly sensed a shift in their conversation and waited for her to explain.

"Well, how would you feel about me joining your family for church after I return from my trip this summer? I know you guys will probably be exhausted after your cruise, but I'd love to see a friendly face when I get there. What do you think?"

Nothing but silence followed.

"You still there, Mel? Did I lose you?"

"No, I'm still here, I'm just trying to process your . . . uh . . . favor. Don't get me wrong, Lisa, I'm thrilled you want to attend church—shocked, really. And of course. We'd love to have you."

"Great!" Lisa said.

"So, what's going on with you?"

"Well, my friend Scott convinced me to start reading the Bible; he's had some major changes in his life, Mel, you just wouldn't believe, and—"

"Wait, so you're doing this all for a guy?"

"I know, but no! I'm not. My intentions may have started out that way, but now I see things in a totally different light."

"Oh, really? I have to hear this; tell me more."

"It's a long story, really. Do you have the time?"

"For you, I'll make the time. Now spill."

Over the next thirty minutes Lisa relayed the events, from her reunion with Scott leading to her new interest in God, her decision to accept Christ, and how everything had impacted her. Melissa couldn't contain the joy of knowing that her best friend had finally come to accept the message she had tried to share with her for so long.

"I'm so happy for you, Lisa," Melissa said. "I can't wait for you to come back and go to church with us. This is the best news ever."

"I know. It's all so new to me. I have so much to learn. Scott even gave me his Bible with all his notes in it. Can you believe that, after all he's been through?"

"Wow, yeah. It sounds like you're not the only one who's had a tough year."

"I know, right? But I still can't believe he didn't tell me about his accident."

"He's a guy! He probably didn't want to seem weak or stupid. Drinking and driving is pretty stupid. He had to be embarrassed."

"I know, but I thought our friendship was different."

"Oh, I don't know, Lisa. Sounds like he really made himself vulnerable. He must care a lot about you to risk telling you everything and even letting you see him in that chair. Most guys wouldn't do that. That's something special."

"You saying you think, maybe, Scott loves me?" Lisa asked, unable to hide her eagerness.

"That's not exactly what I meant. I don't know about love, but there's obviously something special between you two. You've been friends for a long time, and he must really care about you. But love is . . ."

Lisa wasn't listening. Her mind exploded with fantasies about her future with Scott. She knew there was something between them. She'd felt it when they were together. Even the way he looked at her told her everything she needed to know.

Melissa's voice cut through her thoughts. "Lisa, are you listening to me?"

"Huh?"

"That proves my point! Lisa, as much as I'm thrilled that Scott helped you find Jesus, you shouldn't even consider having a that kind of relationship with him right now."

"Why not?" Not her too!

"Well, for starters, it muddles things. As much as you'd like to think you can have that kind of relationship right now, you shouldn't."

"That's stupid; I can't be in love because I've accepted Jesus?"

"That's not what I'm saying. It's just that you need time to grow in your relationship with God, so He can always be first in your life. Scott's been a believer long enough to know that."

"So what does that have to do with anything?"

"You're just beginning a relationship with Jesus, and Scott already has one."

"Are you telling me I'm not religious enough for him?" Lisa's cheeks grew hot as she pressed the cell phone tighter to her ear.

"Not exactly . . ."

"I sense a 'but' coming."

"Fine. Lisa you need to make sure you're doing this for the right reason, for yourself, and that it's not about Scott. You don't want to lose focus on what's most important here. God's shown Himself to you, and I know He has even bigger plans for you. If you don't believe me, check out Jeremiah 29:11."

Lisa didn't know how to respond.

"Lisa, listen, I'm so happy for you, but I'm sorry, I have to go now. My mom needs me to help her with the laundry before bedtime, and she says I've been on the phone long enough. You know how she is about that. I'll talk to you again soon. Text me anytime, okay?"

"I will."

"Love ya."

"Ditto."

Lisa swiped "END" on her phone. This was the second time she'd been warned to proceed carefully in her relationship with Scott. Could there be something to what they were saying? Maybe she should listen. She'd have to think about it for a bit.

Aunt Jane tapped softly on the door. "You about finished, Lisa? That homework isn't going to finish itself."

"Yes, I'm coming. Just give me a couple more minutes." Lisa jumped off the bed and typed the Bible verse Melissa had given her into the search bar on her phone. "Come on," she said, tapping her thumb impatiently on the screen as she waited. Within a minute, multiple websites popped up; she clicked on the first one and read:

"For I know the plans I have for you," declares the Lord, "plans to prosper you and not to harm you, plans to give you hope and a future."

Plans to give me hope and a future, huh? Does that include my parents as well?

"Interesting."

"What's that?" Aunt Jane asked, interrupting her thoughts.

Lisa looked up from her phone to where her aunt waited patiently in the doorway. "Oh, nothing. Melissa just gave me a Bible verse and said I had to look it up. Jeremiah 29:11." Lisa walked toward the doorway. "Oh, and she said she's more than happy to have me join her and her family at church when I return. She's being weird about me and Scott, though."

"How so?" Aunt Jane said, turning and walking toward the stairs in front of Lisa.

"Well, for starters, she knows Scott's been a Christian for a while and is dealing with his own problems. She's concerned as a new Christian I'm not ready for a relationship with him. She's worried I'll lose focus and that a relationship with Scott will be a distraction from God or something."

"Your friend sounds like a very smart young lady. Not many young people think things through these days; they just jump into a relationship and deal with the consequences later. Tell me then, Lisa," Aunt Jane said, as they stepped into the kitchen, "what do you think about having a romantic relationship with Scott?" She walked to the counter and poured herself a cup of coffee.

Lisa sat down at the kitchen table and looked sheepishly at her hands. "I'd be lying if I said the thought hadn't crossed my mind." She looked up at her aunt. "Look, I know how you feel about me pursuing a relationship right now, but I just don't see a problem with it. Why can't I just be happy for once?"

"Oh, honey," Aunt Jane began, slipping into the chair next to Lisa's, "of course, I want you to be happy, but I also care more about what's in your best interest. Melissa does too. Your life has been extremely complicated, and your problems aren't going to go away overnight. You have a lot that needs to be worked out. You really need to focus on that, don't you think?"

She had a point. As much as she'd tried, she'd found it difficult to focus on anything in the past few days without images of Scott's smile filling her mind. Scott had been the one to point her in the right direction; he had a deep concern for her spiritual well-being, just like Melissa. Maybe that was all. Maybe they were just really good friends, and that's all they ever would be. And hadn't he also made it clear they'd be friends and nothing more?

Still, there had been a spark of something between them the last time they had been together, hadn't there? Of course that ended when she became angry and lost her temper. The fact was, she was still angry. But she was quickly starting to regret it.

How immature can you be, Lisa?

It wasn't like they were in *that* kind of relationship. What had made her think Scott owed her any explanation? No wonder he hadn't called! Sighing, Lisa pulled her cell phone from her back pocket. She couldn't just sit and wait for him to call. She had created the problem, now she had to do something about it and prove that she still valued their friendship.

She clicked on Scott's contact in her messaging app and typed.

Scott, I'm sorry about blowing up at you before. . . .

She quickly pressed, "Send" before she could lose her nerve. If he didn't respond, she wasn't sure what she would do.

They just needed to put all this conflict behind them and work on being friends again. He was probably tired of all the drama. Yes, that had to be it. Unless . . .

Maybe he's just tired of me.

No, she couldn't bear to entertain that consequence.

She looked at Aunt Jane. "I think I need to get some air," she said, then jumped up from her chair and raced toward the back door.

"Lisa, wait . . . Where are you going?" Aunt Jane called, rising from her chair. "It's cold outside; you need a sweater."

"It's fine, don't worry; I'll be back," Lisa said as she slipped out of the door. "Soon."

Lisa walked briskly out past the barn, tears stinging her eyes. Soon, she was out by the old oak tree that had once sheltered Ryan's treehouse. She placed her hand on its rough bark and inhaled the fresh night air. Tilting her head back, she looked deep into the night sky.

Hello, Lord, this is Lisa. I'm so confused. I know I've really messed things up down here, especially with Scott. I don't know what your plan is for us or if there is one. But God, I could really use your help.

CHAPTER 23

Outside, in the light of the fading day, Lisa braced herself against the wind and quickly headed into the woods. Yes, what she was doing was a little crazy, but she desperately needed to find Gabe. If anyone knew what the future would bring, he would. He was an angel, after all. Wasn't he?

Lisa slowed her pace when she reached the clearing where they had first met.

Her voice bellowed over the whistling of the wind through the trees. "Hello! Is anyone there? Gabe?"

There was no reply.

Of course. What was she thinking? She'd been crazy to think he would appear to her again just because she needed him. But what was she going to do? Where would she find the answers she needed? She huddled down against an old oak and began to cry.

The wind suddenly settled, and a voice rose gently out of the silence. "We have to stop meeting like this, you know."

Startled, Lisa stood and turned in the direction of the voice. Standing just a few feet away was Gabe.

"Gabe, I'm so glad I found you," she said, taking a step in his direction. "I really need your help."

"Lisa, what's wrong?" Gabe said, hurrying to her side. "Is everything okay with your aunt?"

"Yeah, she's fine. I just needed to talk to you. I need to talk to you about Scott!"

"That's what this is about? Whew! You had me worried there for a second." Gabe took a deep breath, and his stance relaxed. "Well, as flattered as I am, you didn't have to come looking for me to find someone to talk to, you know."

Lisa felt a sudden chill and began rubbing hands together in an attempt to warm herself. "What do you mean?"

"Wait. What am I doing just standing around while you catch a chill? Here, let me create a fire while we chat a bit."

Without another word, Gabe went to work collecting firewood and brush from the forest floor. Lisa watched in awe as he expertly rubbed two sticks together immediately igniting a small flame. Adding more brush to the foundation of the fire, the flames grew higher and brighter. Soon, the two of them were huddled together in silence as they watched the orange flames dance, fighting against the wind.

"I never really realized how beautiful fire can be," Lisa said, breaking the silence.

"It is beautiful, isn't it? It's a shame that not everyone sees His mighty wonders."

"I'm beginning to realize that more and more."

"I'm glad. Now, tell me why you came to find me. You do know I don't have all the answers, right? Only He does." Gabe pointed toward the sky.

"But you *are* an angel, aren't you? My aunt told me I'm not the first one in the family you've visited."

"I'm surprised Jane remembered me; I do my best to deliver God's messages quickly. I like to get in and get out as quickly as possible." He chuckled.

"Well, whatever you said to her made quite the impression, brief or not. She could hardly believe it when I told her I had met you." Gabe added some sticks to the fire and continued watching the flames.

"Well?" she finally said," I need to know what is in the future for me and Scott?"

Gabe looked at her. "I'm sorry to disappoint you, but I can't look into the future. As a messenger of God, I am given a specific message to deliver. Nothing more, nothing less. And I'm here to spread God's love to all of mankind and give people hope." Gabe poked at the fire. "I will tell you this though: the Father is very proud of you. He sees how far you've come and knows how much you've changed in such a short time.

Don't lose sight of that and get caught up in the things of this world. They will never satisfy you."

"But how can I be sure I'm making the right choices? It's one thing to know God it's another to know what he wants me to do."

"That's why it's called faith. It's like the sun shining on a cloudy day. You don't always see it because it's hidden from view by the clouds, but you know it's there. It's the same with God. As you grow in faith, you will learn to recognize Him more and more in your life. Don't turn back now. There's more at stake here than you know."

"What's that supposed to mean?"

Gabe shook his head. "I've said too much already, Lisa. Let's leave things as they are. Your aunt is probably worried sick about you being out in the cold for this long. You should head home now." Gabe nodded his head in the direction that led back home.

"Wait," Lisa said, holding up one hand. "Can you at least tell me this before you go: Am I going to be okay?"

Gabe closed the distance between them and gave her a hug. "You're going to be more than okay, God's got you, and there's no better place to be than in His hands." He smiled, then cast a sidelong glance toward the house. "Go on, now, before she sends a search party."

Lisa looked toward the house and then back at Gabe. "Will I ever see you again?"

"Honestly, I don't know. I go where I'm needed." He tilted his head again toward the house. " I'm not good with goodbyes."

"But this isn't goodbye, is it? I'm sure we'll see each other on the other side. Ri—"

But before she could finish the question, Gabe was gone.

Still, she knew deep down, she'd see him again someday.

Nearly an hour later, Lisa returned to the house. Shivering from the cold, she burst through the kitchen and ran to the living room. She quickly grabbed an Afghan from the couch and wrapped herself in it, then curled up in the chair.

"My goodness, Lisa, what were you thinking?" her aunt chided, several minutes later, setting down her knitting. "Going out there, it's almost dark, and without even a sweater to keep the chill off?"

"I know, I'm sorry. I just had to clear my head. I needed to be alone, to think. Honestly, I didn't even realize I was cold until I came out of the woods. Then I ran as fast as I could to get back here."

"Care to share what's going on in that pretty little head of yours?"

"Maybe later." Lisa said with a smile as she locked her secrets deep in her heart, at least for the time. She unwrapped herself from the afghan and stretched with a huge yawn. "Actually, do you mind if I just go to bed now?"

"That's fine, honey."

"Homework will have to wait till tomorrow. Is that okay?"

"That's fine. I'm sure you could use a good night's sleep. Sweet dreams, honey." Aunt Jane picked up her knitting and set back to work.

Scott had tossed and turned for over an hour, trying to get to sleep, but it was useless—his mind still reeled from the harsh truth. He had allowed everything in his life to get so out of control . . . and for a girl, no less! Rolling onto his side, he switched on his bedside lamp and reached for his phone. With the touch of a button, the blank screen came to life, showing all the notifications he'd missed over the last hour.

As he scrolled down on his phone, the bright blue screen casting an eerie glow around the darkened room. There were the usual annoying reminders to come back and play from his favorite game apps, a reminder for his next doctor's appointment, and the usual spam. The last notification made Scott rise on his elbow, rub his eyes, and pay attention. It was a text message from Lisa. How had he missed it? Clicking on the message with his thumb, he held his breath and read.

Scott, I'm sorry about blowing up at you before. I realize now you were just trying to protect me. But you don't have to do that anymore. I'm a big girl. Let's not spend the rest of this summer fighting, okay? I want my best friend back. Truce? Please call me, or I'll be forced to file a missing person's report soon!

Scott couldn't wait. It was late, but she might be up. If not, she'd see his text first thing in the morning. He quickly typed out a response.

Sorry, I just saw your text. There's no need to file a report! I'm still here. You don't need to apologize. All is forgiven. We both handled things the best we could. Let's just try to move on from here. I want to know what you have been up to . . .

Smiling, he scanned the text one last time as his thumb hovered over the send button.

Did he dare write more?

No, he wouldn't let himself go there—not right now, at least. Still, his heart yearned to echo back the sentiment of her desires . . . like her, he also wanted his best friend back, but voicing his true feelings would only complicate things.

Scott pressed the send button and tossed his cell phone on the nightstand.

Lord, thank you for opening the lines of communication between Lisa and me. I let my emotions get the best of me and forgot why I started this in the first place. Lisa still needs you, Lord.

With that simple prayer, Scott turned off his light and drifted to sleep.

Lisa reached her bedroom and quietly shut the door. She sat on the edge of the bed and slipped her phone out of her pocket. Locating the message icon on her phone, she noted one new text.

It was from Scott.

Reading his text, she frowned; despite its positive nature, she had hoped for something a little more personal. Oh well. It was a start. She should be happy he was still talking to her. Plus, maybe things would change once he found out she'd become a Christian.

Lisa shot off a response.

Scott's cell phone chimed. He slid it from the nightstand and checked the notifications. A new message from Lisa. He quickly opened the message and read.

No problem. But you had me worried there for a minute! I agree. Let's just move on from here. I've been busy with my studies and just hanging out. Aunt Jane and Mike are fighting. I have something important to tell you, but I'd rather tell you in person. When can we meet?

He wasted no time responding.

Ding!
Well, that was fast.
Lisa turned on her side to retrieve her phone from the nightstand, then read the text.

I'm sorry to hear about your aunt. Tell her I'll pray for her. She seemed okay when we last talked."

Ha! So he admitted it. The question was, how many times had he checked up on her through Aunt Jane in the past weeks?

Grinning, Lisa sent off her next text.

Checkin' up on me, were you? ;)

A few minutes passed with no response. Had she gone too far with the flirty wink? After a few more minutes of anxious waiting, she nervously dialed his number. He answered on the first ring.

His gentle laugh came through first, calming Lisa's fears.

"All right, all right," he said. "You caught me; guilty as charged. I just couldn't help myself."

"I knew it!" Lisa said triumphantly.

"I was worried about you, okay? With the way we left things, I thought . . . well, I just wanted to make sure you were okay."

"Hey, I know. Like you said, we both handled things the best we knew how."

"Yes, I realize that now. I just hope you were able to look past my mistakes and truly hear what I had to say."

She chuckled. "Oh, you gave me a lot to think about for sure. So, can we get together and talk? Maybe tomorrow? I really have something I want to tell you." She held her breath.

"Why? You plan on hitting on me again?"

Ouch.

"Sorry," he said. "Forget I said that. It's past one o'clock in the morning, and I'm a little out of it."

"It's okay, I understand. I'm tired myself. So what about tomorrow? I could come over to your house. After lunch, say, around one thirty?"

"That would be great. You sure you don't mind coming this way? "Scott laughed. " I really don't think I can handle those stairs again."

There was that glint of the old Scott again—able to laugh about anything, even at his own expense. She sure loved his sense of humor.

"That's fine," she said, smiling. "Don't worry about it."

"I guess I'll see you tomorrow then. Can't wait to hear your news. I hope it has something to do with—"

"Nope. No guesses. You'll just have to wait and see."

"All right. See you tomorrow, then. Sleep well."

"You too. Goodnight."

Lisa hung up the phone, then fell back onto her bed and squealed with joy. The conversation felt good. He was even joking with her again. The rest would come in time, she was sure of it. Especially once she told him her news.

Tomorrow couldn't come soon enough!

Scott stared at his phone in disbelief. He'd done it again. As happy as he was to be speaking to Lisa again, he'd let his guard down a bit too much. And now she had news she needed to share with him in person tomorrow? Was she going to tell him how she felt about him?

"Forgive me, Lord," he prayed aloud. "I hope she doesn't read too much into our conversation; the last thing I want to do is lead her on."

The truth was, he was still battling his own feelings for her. But he understood now that taking their relationship to the next level was the wrong choice. At least for now. He needed to be ready before she came tomorrow. He needed to have a plan for how he would respond.

Scott rested his head back on the pillow and fell asleep.

Scott groaned at the sunlight streaming through his window. The day had come too quickly, and he still didn't know how to decline Lisa's growing affections without breaking her heart. He'd been foolish thinking he could share so much with her without personal feelings getting involved. The woman she was becoming had been more than he was prepared for. He had to find a way to deal with that. If there were any hope for a relationship in the future, they'd both have to let go of their need for someone else to fill the voids. No, they had too much to work on individually right now. She needed to find her identity in Christ, and He needed to continue to grow in his trust in God above anything else. If that meant keeping his distance for a while, so be it.

He sure had made a mess of things. And not only with Lisa, but his actions had affected his family too. They'd watched him become more withdrawn, losing focus on things that mattered the most. That would change today. Today, he was determined to make things right with both Lisa and his family.

"What will it be today, boys?" Scott's dad said. "A wrestling competition or Legos?" The two McCarthy twins sat around the kitchen table, their breakfasts eaten, while their father nursed the last of his coffee.

"Actually," Scott said, wheeling into the kitchen, "I think they'd much rather spend the morning with me practicing their free throws."

"What do you say boys?" his dad said.

"Yay!" Devon and Marcel shouted in unison.

"Well, I guess that settles it. Come on then, boys," he said, rising from the table. "We'll get things set up in the driveway while Scott has his breakfast." He winked at Scott. "We'll meet you out there when you're finished."

The boys pushed their chairs back from the table and ran for the front door.

Ten minutes later, Scott watched as Devon and Marcel passed the ball to each other.

"That's right. You got it. Remember what I taught you. Hold the ball with both hands, and when you're ready, just flick your wrist like so." Scott demonstrated, tossing an imaginary ball into the air.

He hadn't really thought about it much lately, but he'd missed these times with his brothers. They'd grown up so much this summer, without him noticing. He'd been such an idiot, spending all his time daydreaming about Lisa and ignoring his family.

Scott turned to his dad. "What do you say about little two-on-two—me and you against the boys?" He maneuvered his chair below the hoop.

"I don't know. You think they're ready for it?" He winked at Scott.

"We'll try and take it easy on them," Scott said. "In fact, let's let them shoot first."

A friendly basketball game ensued, and father and son helped the boys score several points against them by purposely missing tosses and hoisting them into the air to make shots. Despite Scott's limitations, he found himself surprised by his ability to twirl his chair around and make some difficult shots.

He tossed another shot over his shoulder and straight into the basket.

"Way to go, Scotty," his dad said, high-fiving him. "On that note, let's take a break."

Scott wheeled toward the edge of the driveway, and his father plopped himself down on the grass in front of him, while Devon and Marcel ran after the ball.

"You know what?" Scott said. "I've missed this." He turned to Devon and Marcel as they ran up to join them. "I'm sorry I haven't been there for you guys lately. I lost my focus and forgot what was important." He pointed at his brothers. "And that's you two troublemakers!" He laughed. "I hope you guys can forgive me?"

"Thank you, son, for the apology, but it's not necessary. We're your family. We love you no matter what. Right, boys?"

"Yeah!" the boys shouted, and then clambered around Scott's wheelchair for a group hug.

CHAPTER 24

"Lisa! Lisa!"

Lisa braced herself as Marcel and Devon ran full speed down the driveway toward her. She crouched, ready for impact, then wrapped them both in a hug. "Oh, wow! Did you miss me?" She laughed, steadying herself to keep from falling.

"Where ya been, Lisa?" Marcel said as she straightened to regain her balance.

"Yeah, how come you don't visit anymore?" Devon grabbed her left hand, Marcel her right, and the two pulled her up the driveway toward the house.

Lisa glanced, with feigned desperation, toward Scott, who sat under the basketball net. Mr. McCarthy stood next to him. She smiled at them both as Devon and Marcel continued their interrogation.

"Welcome back, Lisa," Mr. McCarthy said when she reached them.

"Enough with the questions, boys. It's time to go inside. I'm sure Lisa will have more time for you a little later."

"But Dad . . ." the boys shouted in unison.

"No, but's," he said, ushering the boys away from her. "You heard me. Let's go."

Lisa stood silently next to Scott, watching the trio walk inside. After a few moments of silence, Scott turned to her.

"How about we go sit on the deck and talk?" Scott said.

Lisa nodded, then walked beside him as he led the way toward the deck. He motioned to a blue-flowered rattan chair under the shade of the tall birch tree. Lisa sat.

"Devon and Marcel sure missed you," Scott said, wheeling his chair across from her.

"I know. They've grown like weeds since I saw them last."

"You should see them play basketball together; they've actually learned the point is to pass the ball instead of hogging it all to themselves." Scott laughed.

"Oh, really? Maybe you and I can play them in a little two-on-two some time." She flashed him a quick smile.

"Yeah. You know I'm really not half bad, even in this chair."

After several awkward moments, Lisa broke the silence.

"I'm a Christian!"

Finally, after weeks of silence, she had shared her secret with him.

A huge grin spread across Scott's face. "Lisa, that's great! I've been praying all this time that you'd read the Bible and come to know Christ."

"Yeah, well, I thought a lot about what you said and then I did start reading the Bible you gave me."

"And?"

"Then I went to church with Aunt Jane, and right there in the pew, I accepted Christ. I'm just beginning to understand it all, and I'm learning to put my trust in God instead of myself. As you know, I have a very strong sense of independence."

"Here, here!" Scott laughed, raising an imaginary glass in celebratory.

"Which brings me to the second reason I'm here: I'm hoping you'll be interested in studying the book of John with me while I'm in town. I could really use your knowledge; being a new Christian, there is so much I don't understand. What do you say?"

Lisa smiled coyly. It was true; she could use Scott's help in making sense of everything. Of course, it would be even better if it helped them reconnect. She wouldn't force things, but she didn't want things to continue the way they were. If there was going to be something more than friendship between them, maybe this could be the start. The rest would be in the Lord's hands.

"As thrilled as I am with your news, Lisa, I don't know if that's the best idea for us right now."

He eased his chair backward, almost imperceptibly. But Lisa saw it.

"You're saying it's a possibility then," Lisa said, then forced a light laugh.

"I don't know . . . well . . . no." He shook his head. "You're missing my point here, Lisa."

"Explain it to me then, Scott. Why can't we even study together? What are you so afraid of? Do you really think God would bring me this far only to keep us apart?"

"Don't you see, Lisa? God isn't keeping us apart. I'm just trying to make the best choices I can for us."

"So, what's the problem with us studying together then?"

"I'm afraid we'll let our feelings get in the way, and it won't be about studying."

"Would that be so bad?" Lisa stood, closing the distance between them.

"That's just the thing," Scott said, his voice becoming firm. "I don't want it to be about us, and I can't be a distraction for you."

"What do you mean?"

"This time is too important, Lisa. I can see that God is moving in your life, and it's amazing. This is the time you need to build a strong relationship with Him; He's going to become very real to you in the coming months."

"So?"

"So, don't you see? I can't be in the middle of that. I won't."

"But you wouldn't be, I promise."

"But I already am! When God laid sharing my testimony with you on my heart, I thought it was going to be so simple, but I was wrong. Somewhere along the way, I started having these feelings for you and losing focus."

"I don't see a problem with that."

"That's exactly the problem. You're a new Christian; everything seems possible to you. And there's nothing wrong with that. But God needs to build a strong foundation in your life so that you're prepared for the challenges life is going to throw at you. You need to grow in your love for Him. That's got to be your first priority."

Scott took a deep breath, and then continued, his voice softer now. "There will come a time when your faith will be tested, just like mine was last summer, and the closer you are to God, the easier it will be for you.

In fact, everything that has happened between us has only reminded me that God still has a lot of work to do on me as well."

"What exactly are you saying, Scott? That we can't be friends?"

"No, not at all. If this summer has taught me anything, it's that I love being your friend, and I need to do a better job at it."

"So where does that leave us, then?"

"As friends." He threw up his hands. "Just like always."

They were silent for a minute. Lisa looked away, feeling suddenly ashamed.

"Look, Lisa. I know how much you were hoping for more to develop this summer, but that's all I can give you right now."

She looked back at him. "But you just said you have feelings—"

"I know what I said! Look, Lisa, I've handled this summer poorly, and I believe God is allowing us to start fresh; I'm not going to take this second chance for granted."

"But what about—"

"No but's." He held up his hand. "I care about you, Lisa, and I know what's right for us now, and I'm not going to let my feelings change that. Or yours. As much as you may want more in our relationship right now, you're not ready—we're not ready."

"I thought you kids would like a soda." Mr. McCarthy stepped out of the sliding glass doors carrying two glasses. "It's gotten pretty hot out here."

Lisa felt suddenly exposed and frustrated by the interruption.

"Thanks, Dad. How did you know?"

Mr. McCarthy handed a glass to Scott, and then turned to Lisa. "Here, Lisa. You must be thirsty, too."

Lisa took the drink, avoiding eye contact with Mr. McCarthy. She was afraid he'd see that she was upset and started asking questions.

"Okay, well, let me know if you need anything else, kids." He patted Scott on the shoulder, and then retreated into the house.

"I think it's time I go, Scott," Lisa said, not looking up at him.

"Lisa, please trust me in this. It's not easy for me either. I really do care for you."

"Sure. I heard what you said. I just don't agree. But obviously there's nothing I can say that will change things."

Lisa sat her glass on the table and got up. "Well, I guess maybe I'll see you around then."

"Lisa . . ."

Lisa ignored him and hurried back to the driveway, fighting back tears. She wouldn't give Scott the satisfaction of seeing her break down. She hopped in the truck and closed the door, hoping to shut out all that had just happened. She reached for the glove compartment, and then rummaged blindly, through blurry eyes, for a napkin or anything to wipe her tear-stained face. As she did, an assortment of papers fell to the floor.

"I've got to get out of here."

She left the mess for later, quickly turning on the truck and throwing it into gear. She needed to get back to the comfort of Aunt Jane's and put distance between her, Scott, and this whole situation.

On the drive back to Aunt Jane's, Lisa managed to calm herself. She didn't want her to see how upset she was. After all, she'd warned Lisa that a relationship with Scott would be a mistake. The last thing she wanted to hear was, "I told you so."

She sat in the driveway for only a minute before deciding to pick up the papers that had fallen out of the glove box. Her dad wouldn't be happy if she lost any of his paperwork. Twisting her body to reach them, she saw the brown envelope that Melissa's mother had given her, the one Ryan had gotten at Vacation Bible School. She'd completely forgotten about it. Stuffing the other papers in the glove box, she took her brother's envelope and headed into the house.

Aunt Jane sat at the table sipping a cup of tea.

"You're back early."

"Yes, but I really don't want to talk about it right now. Maybe later, okay? I'm just going to go upstairs for a while."

"Of course, Lisa."

Lisa headed up the stairs, Ryan's envelope in hand. Somehow it gave her comfort to have a piece of him with her. Even if it were only a few drawings he'd done.

She sat on the bed and flipped open the envelope. Slowly she pulled out the first paper, expecting to see a crayon drawing or an arts-and-crafts project.

"Oh, Ryan!" Her hand flew to her mouth. "I don't believe this!" She raced back down the stairs so quickly that she stumbled and almost fell halfway down. She regained her balance, and then ran into the kitchen.

"Aunt Jane, look at this! Look at this!"

Aunt Jane took the page and read it out loud.

"On this day, July 14, 2001, Ryan Daniel Sanchez has accepted Jesus as his personal Savior." Tears filled her aunt's eyes. "Oh, Lisa. You see? God loved Ryan just as much as he loves you. Ryan is in heaven with Uncle Frank now."

The two sat silently for several minutes, looking at the certificate.

"This has turned out to be a wonderful day after all," Lisa said.

CHAPTER 25

It had been a few days since Lisa's visit with Scott, and she still hadn't said much about it to Aunt Jane. She had tried to stay positive and enjoy the news that her little brother had accepted Jesus. She only wished she had known before. But as the two of them sat together at the table over dinner, the weight of her talk with Scott continued to occupy her mind.

She'd shared the news of her own salvation with Scott, but it hadn't changed anything. He'd still rejected her, and she still couldn't understand why. She'd become a Christian. Wasn't that enough for him?

Daughter, you are more than enough. You are mine.

The strong admonishment came and went quickly.

Lisa winced. She'd been such a fool to think everything would change when she became a Christian or that this summer was supposed to be about her and Scott.

"Penny, for your thoughts," Aunt Jane said, passing a plate of potatoes at dinner that night.

"Well," Lisa said, drawing herself out of deep thought, "since you asked. Things didn't go well at Scott's the other day; he doesn't want anything more than friendship with me. At least not now." She took a breath. "I don't understand his reasoning, but that's that."

"Oh, honey, I'm so sorry."

"No, it's okay, really. I didn't get it at first, but I'm starting to understand. I shouldn't have pushed for a relationship we're both clearly not ready for. But you know how I can be—stubborn and strong-willed."

"That you are, my dear," Aunt Jane said, stifling a laugh. "So you said you're not ready for that kind of relationship? What makes things so different now?"

"Well, I'm reading I Corinthians 13, and it's drastically changing how I view love. It isn't just some romantic feeling between two people who are physically attracted to one another. Putting someone's needs before your own is a deliberate choice. Scott's done that for me; he's given me a gift—the gift of time. Time to learn more about God and more about myself. If this summer has taught me anything, it's that time is precious and should not be wasted. We both have some work to do before we even think about getting involved with each other. Now," she said, eyeing Aunt Jane, "as for you and Mike . . . that's another story."

"Aww, honey. You don't have to worry about me."

"But I do worry about you. You live all by yourself here with no one to help you with the farm. Not only that, but you've sacrificed your entire summer to help me get my life straightened out—schoolwork and all. Look at the way I've treated you. I took all my problems out on you. I'm so sorry." She reached across the table and took her aunt's hand.

"There's no need to apologize, dear." Aunt Jane said, her fork paused over her plate.

"You don't understand. I feel terrible about the way I reacted to your relationship. I should never have judged Mike like that. You deserve a second chance at love, and I may have ruined it for you. I'd like us to invite him over for dinner one night. To apologize. I owe him that. What do you think?"

"I appreciate your sentiment, Lisa. But you're not the only one who's been confused and made some mistakes this summer. I'm not even sure if he'll want to talk to me after all that's happened."

"Oh, come on, where's that forgiveness stuff you're always talking about? Come on. What have you got to lose?" Lisa said.

"Well . . . I guess it wouldn't hurt to try. I'll give him a call after dinner."

Thirty minutes after dinner, Jane emerged from the bedroom with a girlish smile.

"You were right, Lisa. Mike was so understanding and forgiving. He's coming over tomorrow night for dinner."

"That's great. What did I tell you? Maybe he's wise about some things after all.

Jane's eyes widened.

"What?" Lisa smiled at her aunt innocently. "Look. I know I may have given Mike the 'tough act,' but he was right about some things. Like how we don't need to do things on our own all the time, and that it's okay to let people in. Now, if you'll excuse me, I have some serious studying to do." Lisa smiled as she headed toward the bedroom.

Summer was almost over. It was only days before Lisa would leave Aunt Jane's and head home.

She sat at the desk in her room, finishing up the last make-up paper for science. Lifting her focus from her textbook, Lisa stared out her bedroom window at the glorious sunset on display. As the sun lowered in the distance, the bright orange glow gave way to a deep red color. Before long, it had disappeared over the horizon, its faint shadow casting an eerie glow on the neighbors' cornfields. Why she hadn't stopped to notice sunsets on the farm until recently was beyond her. She hadn't really taken the time to appreciate God's creation for what it was—a masterpiece for all to see.

She was also seeing herself in a new light these days. Like the sunset, God had created her for a purpose. She didn't exactly know what that was yet, but she was sure God would show her eventually. In the meantime, she would continue spending time each day in the Word and the other materials Scott had given her. As part of her daily devotional, she continued to make her way through both 1 and 2 Corinthians.

Today, she'd read II Corinthians 5. The first few verses reminded her of the new body she would receive once she entered heaven. The chapter continued, explaining how our priorities should shift after a spiritual transformation. This was a gentle reminder to her not get stuck in the past because she was "a new creation." The passage continued by saying, "the old has gone; the new is here!" This simple verse reassured her that even though she was bound to make mistakes from time to time, she could always count on the fact that God was with her, even when she overreacted, and His Spirit convicts us when we are wrong.

Like with Scott. And Mike. Why did she react so strongly when they were around?

You care so deeply for your friends and your loved ones. They matter to you, just like you matter to me.

Lisa allowed the words to settle deep within her heart. Until now, she'd never considered herself a reflection of God's love in the world.

I'm sorry, Lord. I know I haven't done the greatest job of showing your love to those around me. I'm so used to letting my emotions have control; please, show me a different way to live.

She'd done her best to reach out to Scott and apologize, but what she'd managed to do instead was once again lose control of her emotions. She'd practically thrown herself at him, revealing her feelings for him and almost demanding he love her back. He'd wavered for only a second but explained the reasons they couldn't be together. He'd been so patient with her, explaining that this in no way erased their connection. Instead, it strengthened it. After all, they were brothers and sisters in Christ now; nothing would ever change that.

Still, he hadn't dismissed the idea of a relationship in the future. That gave her hope for them yet. Though he'd admitted his feelings for her, he'd chosen to lay them down for the greater good of her finding Jesus. But why? Try as she might, Lisa couldn't completely understand his reasoning. She appreciated the time he'd spent with her, and she had grown through it. Now he wouldn't even study the Bible with her. He'd made his decision clear—that didn't mean she had to like it.

Why couldn't they grow in God together? The question nagged, even as she worked to complete her assignments from school.

The next night, once Mike had left the house after a successful reconciliation with Aunt Jane, Lisa went upstairs to her room to do some Bible reading before bed. She was trying hard to stay focused on the words, despite her mind wandering back constantly to the giddiness she'd witnessed on Aunt Jane and Mike's faces and wishing she could experience the same thing with Scott. But when she came to Matthew 6:24, she was stopped in her tracks:

No one can serve two masters. Either you will hate one and love the other, or you will be devoted to one and despise the other. You cannot serve both God and money.

Wait. Was that what she was doing? Trying to have her cake and eat it too?

Stunned, she rushed out of her room to seek Jane's interpretation of the verse. After listening to Lisa's concerns, she reached for her phone.

"Here's what the Living Bible translation says." She opened a Bible app on her phone and typed in the reference. "Let's see if it makes it any clearer for you. It reads as follows: 'You cannot serve two masters; God and money. For you will hate one and love the other, or else the other way around.' Now I know, in this instance, they are talking about God and the love of wealth, but I guess you could substitute other sins as well."

"So God's asking me to choose what's more important?"

"Yes, that's what Jesus wants for all His children—for them to choose Him above themselves every day. I know this may be difficult for you as a new Christian to understand, but you will in time."

"Great. What does God expect me to do in the meantime? Become a nun?"

Aunt Jane fought back a chuckle. "No. Of course not. I'm just saying God wants to have first priority in your life in whatever path you choose. He wants to see His fingerprints on everything you do. Let me read you something from Colossians 3:23 and 24." She typed in her phone again then read. "It says, 'Whatever you do, work at it with all your heart, as working for the Lord, not for human masters, since you know that you will receive an inheritance from the Lord as a reward. It is the Lord Christ you are serving.'"

"So, I can choose my future, and He will bless it? Is that what you're saying?"

"Yes and no. God can take our circumstances and bless them if He wants, but that won't necessarily be His automatic response. Take Uncle Frank's heart attack, for example. I would have loved nothing more than for him to recover and be with me. But that's not how God chose to resolve things. Instead, I am learning a whole new type of reliance on God for my needs. During hard times, we learn the most about the Lord, His character, and ourselves as a whole."

"I don't know. I know I still have a lot to learn, but it all seems kind of backward to me."

"That's just the thing. It is backward. Not only does God want us to focus on loving and serving others, but He wants us to examine our motives for doing things as well."

Lisa raised her eyebrows. "Huh?"

"Sorry, dear. Sometimes, I forget who I'm talking to and don't know how to break down the concepts into understandable language." Jane slowly tapped her chin with a finger, and then tried again. "Let's see, where do I start?"

"At the very start of His thirty years of ministry on earth, Jesus was disappointed to learn how much of Scripture had been taken out of context and misused to suit mankind's interest. He saw firsthand how the high priests took their spiritual knowledge for granted. Instead of using it to point others to the Lord, they began to think of themselves as role models, taking the Bible and the Ten Commandments to condemn rather than instruct. They soon began looking down on others instead of loving them as God commanded."

"Wow."

"That's exactly what Jesus thought. He was disappointed at how easily the people had strayed from God and given into their own self-righteousness. He desired to help them return to the Father, rebuilding on the foundation of faith they'd once held dear. More than anything, though, He just wanted to heal people from their physical and spiritual wounds."

"So, what happened?"

"As you can imagine, Jesus' ministry received mixed reviews. Some recognized His miracles and immediately acknowledged Him for who He was—their awaited Savior. As a result, they repented of their sins and were more than happy to accept this new way of living and to drop everything to follow Jesus. Others, though, wanted nothing to do with Him, refusing to accept what was right in front of them; some even went as far as to say that Jesus was possessed. So set in their ways, most religious leaders were unwilling to consider a moral standard besides their own. Still, some struggled to work the system, acknowledging the miracles, yet refusing to take sides and turn from their old ways."

"How did Jesus respond to all this?"

"He just kept on loving people."

"Wow, that's amazing, considering everything He was up against," Lisa said, "I'm surprised he didn't speak out more."

"Right? Now, that doesn't mean he didn't get angry from time to time and stand behind the Word God gave him to preach. But, eventually, He would turn the religious leaders on their heads by teaching the Beatitudes."

"The Beatitudes? What are they?"

"The Beatitudes were part of one of the most popular sermons of Jesus' earthly ministry. In it, He attempted to inspire believers to start living for the kingdom of heaven instead of this world and all its earthly treasures. He urged them not to lose hope, reminding them God's standards are nothing like the worlds. Contrary to what they had been taught, it wasn't just about how much they'd done to further the kingdom so much as the state of their heart in the process. Let me read you some examples, starting with Matthew 5:3–5." Again, she entered a new reference into the app, then continued. "It says: 'Blessed are the poor in spirit, for theirs is the kingdom of heaven. Blessed are those who mourn, for they will be comforted. Blessed are the meek, for they will inherit the earth.'"

"Wow." Lisa let out a breath. "Those are drastically different than today's societal standards."

"That's exactly what I'm getting it. God's standards are different than ours."

"I really do still have a lot to learn."

"Don't worry. That's why you have Melissa, me, and Scott to turn to if you have questions."

Scott hesitated for a moment, and then picked up his cell phone. Over the last few days, he'd received several texts from Lisa, apologizing for her behavior and asking him to call her back. As much as he cared for her, he hoped a little time and distance would benefit them both. This would give him time to repair things with his family and, hopefully, allow Lisa to reevaluate her priorities and put everything into perspective.

Until that day, Scott hadn't really known how serious her feelings for him were, and now that he had, he wasn't quite sure how to proceed. Because of it, he'd remained silent, taking time to respond to her, fearing his rush to respond would only encourage her.

He stopped, thumbs hovered over his phone's screen.

What should I do, Lord? How do I navigate this mess?

He sighed. He'd spent much time since she left that afternoon reflecting on his conversations with her. He still couldn't forgive himself for losing focus and letting his emotions cloud his judgment. As a result, he'd completely missed the truth, staring him in the face—he wasn't the only one battling feelings; Lisa was in love with him.

Making matters even worse, he'd admitted his feelings for her! He groaned. How was he supposed to come back from that?

Lisa continued to fight disappointment with herself. She'd been unfair to Scott in so many ways, first in how she had reacted when he told her about his accident and then when she had pushed him for a more intimate relationship. She knew it was difficult for him and that he had growing feelings for her, yet she had disregarded his own struggle to do the right thing and demanded more from him.

She had thought a lot about his reasons and had also been thinking about some of the things she had read in her Bible. She had spent a lot of time reading the book of 1 Corinthians in the Bible Scott had given her, and she was learning about true love—the agape kind of love. In chapter 13, she read:

Love is patient, love is kind. It does not envy, it does not boast, it is not proud. It does not dishonor others, it is not self-seeking, it is not easily angered, it keeps no record of wrongs. Love does not delight in evil but rejoices with the truth. It always protects, always trusts, always hopes, always perseveres.

These qualities of love were so far beyond anything she had ever imagined. She wasn't ready to give that kind of love. She had a long way to go before she would be.

If she and Scott were ever to be together, she needed to learn how to love. First, how to love God, then to love herself again, and finally, someday, to love someone else.

CHAPTER 26

"What on earth are you doing up so late?" Aunt Jane yawned as she shuffled into the kitchen wrapped in her bathrobe, her furry pink slippers sliding across the floor. "You have a long drive ahead of you tomorrow. The last thing we need on the road is a sleepy head."

"I'm sorry, Aunt Jane. I just couldn't sleep. I hope I didn't wake you. I'm excited about going home, but I'm also nervous about seeing my parents."

"I understand. But remember, you're not going home alone. God is going with you, and He sees your commitment and your faith. He will honor that. I must admit, though, I'm a little anxious too." Aunt Jane kissed Lisa on the forehead, then shuffled over to the coffee maker. She stopped and turned back to Lisa. "As much as I'd love a cup of coffee, I'd never get back to sleep. How about a hot cup of tea?"

"Sounds good."

Aunt Jane filled the teakettle and retrieved a tin of tea from the cupboard. Setting the kettle on the stove to brew, she joined Lisa at the table.

"So, what are you anxious about, Aunt Jane?" Lisa asked, looking at her intently.

"Honestly, I'm concerned about your mother. Let's not forget why she sent you here. She expected me to supervise you and make sure you complete all your studies. I'm not sure how she'll take the fact that I'm sending you back 'religious,' so to speak."

"The change is that obvious?"

"Yes, Lisa. You may not recognize it, but others can see it. They may not know what to call it, but there's lightness within your spirit that wasn't there before. It's like the apostle Paul says in 2 Corinthians 5:17: 'Therefore, if anyone is in Christ, the new creation has come: the old has gone, the new is here!' The difference is night and day."

"And you're worried about how my mother will take the news that I'm a Christian?"

"Heavens, yes," Aunt Jane said, rising at the sound of the whistling teakettle. "Your mother has been very clear about how she feels about my religion. It's changed our relationship. We were remarkably close growing up, you know. She was my best friend; we did everything together. We even lived together after high school before I married your uncle. But things became different between us after I got married and gave my life to Jesus. Not only did she feel she was being replaced by your uncle, but as I leaned more into my faith and began trying to share it with her, the distance between us grew greater."

"I guess that explains why Mom never wants to go to church. We only go on special occasions, and, even then, generally Dad takes us."

"I guess it does." Aunt Jane returned to the table with two steaming cups and sat next to Lisa. "Your mother wasn't interested in my Jesus. Once, she got so upset with me, she threatened to stop visiting and end your summer visits if I continued sharing my 'religious obsession,' as she called it, with you."

"So that's why you stopped talking about God and Jesus when we visited? I always wondered why Mom used to give you such a stern look when the subject of faith came up."

Aunt Jane nodded. "I love your mother, but she was adamant about it and can be quite stubborn. Just like someone else I know."

"Who, me?" Lisa laughed, giving her aunt a playful look. "I guess it was a surprise, then, when she agreed to let me come this summer. But she knows you're taking me to church and hasn't said anything about it. At least not to me."

"Nor to me, but I'm very grateful she did allow you to come. It has given me to chance to be with you at one of the most important times of your life."

"Me too."

The two sat in silence, sipping their tea, a sense of ease between them. When the clock in the living room chimed one o'clock, they said good night and headed to bed.

Aunt Jane was in the kitchen wiping the counters clean when Lisa came down the following day.

"Morning, Aunt Jane. You're a busy bee this morning. I'm surprised you're up already after our late night."

"Believe me, I didn't want to be." Aunt Jane chucked. "I just needed to pick things up before everyone arrives for lunch. You didn't forget, did you?"

"Gosh, I totally forgot everyone was coming over today. Is it too late to cancel and promise to catch them the next time I visit?" Lisa asked jokingly. She took down a mug and poured a cup of coffee.

"You'd better be kidding? You know, they're coming specifically to see you off. Like it or not, you are part of the family of God now, and they want to send you off in prayer."

"Of course, I'd love to say goodbye to everyone. I'll take a quick shower before they arrive." Lisa kissed her aunt on the cheek. "So," she said, turning back from the doorway, coffee in hand, "who'd you invite, anyway?" She hoped Scott would be there, but they hadn't talked in the last few weeks, and she wasn't sure where they stood.

"There are a couple of the ladies from the Monday Bible study, Sara and Helen; Lily from church—oh, and Mike, of course."

"What about Scott?" Lisa asked, half regretting the words as soon as they came out. "You invited him, right?"

"Oh, honey, of course I invited him. I left a message at the McCarthy house and on his cell phone, but I haven't heard back."

"I texted him yesterday, but haven't heard back either." Lisa sighed. "Honestly, I don't know where we stand, and I hate going home with things the way they are between us."

"He's probably just been busy and forgot to reply. You know how boys can be. I'm sure that's all there is to it. Now hurry up and get showered." She shooed Lisa along with her hands. "I hope you're all packed."

"Yes, I'm all packed. And I certainly hope you're right about Scott."

"He will probably just surprise you and simply show up. Now, go!"

Lisa turned and hurried up the stairs, praying her Aunt Jane was right.

Turning off the hairdryer, Lisa stared at her reflection in the mirror. She looked much the same as she did the first day she arrived. But, yes, there were changes; the inner changes had softened the deep frown lines from her brow, and her eyes sparkled with renewed excitement for life and what it would bring. While so much of the future was still uncertain and she still didn't have all the answers, she knew God did, and that made all the difference.

Brushing out her soft brown curls, she added a touch of blush and lip color. Pulling on a pair of comfortable black leggings and slipping on a glitzy black tunic top, she viewed herself in the full-length mirror on the back of her door. She needed to dress comfortably for the long drive ahead, but she still wanted to look her best, just in case Scott showed.

"Hey, son. You have a minute?" Scott's dad peeked around his bedroom doorframe.

"Of course, Dad," Scott said, backing up his wheelchair from the desk and motioning his dad to the bed. "Have a seat. Is something wrong?"

"Oh, no, nothing like that," his father said, sitting on the bed. "Your mother and I just wanted to tell you how proud we are of you and all your progress this summer. We know it hasn't been easy dealing with Lisa, but you showed maturity in slowing things down. Despite the difficulties in your relationship, you shared your faith with her, and you grew spiritually in the process."

"Thanks, Dad. Doing my best."

"I can't tell you how happy I am to see you reading your Bible and getting back into church."

"Thanks, Dad . . . why do I sense a 'but' coming?"

"You're smart, son." His father chuckled. "And you're right; we do have some concerns. Your mother and I don't want you to look back on this summer with Lisa with regrets. While we are confident in the advice we gave you, we're worried you may have gotten the idea that we wouldn't approve of a relationship between the two of you in the future. She's an amazing young woman, and now that she is a believer, who knows—maybe God's plan is for the two of you to be together."

"Wait a minute. What exactly are you saying?" Scott felt the frustration rising in his voice. He took a breath and tried to rein it in. "Dad, I told her I didn't want a romantic relationship. Isn't that what you wanted? Now you want me to take back everything I said to her? I can't do that. I really hurt her. I'm not even sure she would ever want that kind of relationship with me now."

"Easy, son. You need to listen carefully to what I am saying." He reached forward and placed his hand on Scott's shoulder. "It's just that, we didn't expect you to take it to this extreme. We advised you to be careful when interacting with her, to give her the time to grow in her relationship with the Lord. Now we're concerned you're completely ignoring her and her friendship." He eased back on the bed. "We know Lisa's been trying to reach out to you, and Mrs. Mitchell has called here as well. You haven't responded to either of them, have you?"

Scott shook his head.

"Scott, Lisa is leaving. You need to have things right between you before she does." His father looked at him sympathetically. "You don't want to miss this opportunity to say goodbye."

Scott's shoulders dropped. "I know. She's left several messages on my phone."

"I'm sure she wants her friend back. So what's stopping you from returning her call?"

"I don't know. I guess I'm afraid. I don't know where we go from here. I know I'm not ready for a serious relationship, but I don't want to lose her either, Dad." He threw up his hands in frustration. "I don't know what to do."

"So tell her that. You and I both know there's something more between you. Doing nothing is just a copout. You're stronger than that, Scott.

"She's not ready for that, Dad. And neither am I. I don't want to confuse her again."

"I wouldn't be so quick to judge. You've both grown a lot this summer. Lisa is growing in her faith, and you recognize you have more potential for your life than you ever imagined."

"But what if—"

"You can't live your life on 'what if's' son. But I guarantee you, if you don't tell her goodbye, you'll regret it. By now, Lisa probably realizes she put you in an awkward position before and wants to make things right between you."

"You think so?"

"I do." Mr. McCarthy said, "the going away get-together is today at noon." He placed a handwritten phone message on Scott's desk, and then glanced at his watch. "You need to decide, and it's getting a little late. It's your decision. I can take you if—"

"Give me twenty minutes, and I'll be ready."

His dad smiled. "Sure thing. I'll pull the car around and meet you out front." He stood and walked to the door, then turned back. "Son, I'm proud of you and the man you're becoming."

"Thanks, Dad. I really appreciate it."

Once his father left, Scott put on his favorite blue polo shirt, brushed his hair, and looked at his reflection. His dad was right. He and Lisa were different now. He needed to see her. He needed to say goodbye. What came next was anyone's guess.

Before long, Scott heard the familiar toot of the car horn. He glanced in the mirror one last time, then made a U-turn with his wheelchair and headed out the bedroom door.

"So what's the plan, son?"

Scott turned to his father in the driver's seat. They'd arrived minutes before at the Mitchell farm, but Scott hadn't made a move to get out. He was frozen, trying to prepare himself for Lisa's reaction. Would she be happy to see him? What would he say to her?

"Do you want me to hang around, or will you call me when you want to come home?"

Scott didn't respond.

"Hello . . ." Scott's dad waved his hand in front of his face. "Earth to Scott. Are you nervous?"

"Not sure nervous even begins to cover it. I'm petrified."

"Would you like me to say a prayer?"

"Sure, Dad. I think that might help."

Lisa sat on the porch watching Mr. McCarthy's car, waiting for the passenger door to open. Her heart had nearly jumped out of her chest when she saw the car pull up. Was Scott really here? She could barely believe her eyes.

It seemed like an eternity before Scott's dad finally retrieved the wheelchair from the back and reassembled it. The rest of the guests were already assembled out on the lawn, where Aunt Jane had set up a lovely picnic. After a couple of minutes, Scott wheeled himself to the front porch, his father following behind.

Lisa immediately stood and walked toward them.

"Are you going to need me to rescue you from these steps again?" The biggest smile was stretched across her face.

Scott laughed. "Nope. Dad's here this time."

"I'm so glad you came," Lisa said. "I've really missed you."

"I've missed you too."

Mr. McCarthy helped Scott up the steps and onto the porch. "I think that does it. Anything else I can do for you kids?"

"Appreciate it, Dad. Why don't you go mingle? I'm sure Lisa's aunt would love to see you."

"Of course. You two have fun."

"You too," Lisa said, "And thanks for bringing Scott all this way."

Mr. McCarthy waved as he descended the stairs and walked to where the other adults were gathered in the garden. Moments later, the group erupted in laughter. Mr. McCarthy had apparently already started with his jokes.

"Dad will keep them entertained, I'm sure," Scott said, turning toward Lisa with a smile. "So, how have you been?"

"Good," she said, nervousness again rising in her chest. "Mike and Aunt Jane have patched things, as you can see." She gestured to the two standing together, arm in arm. "He's a really good guy. Aunt Jane is the happiest she's ever been."

That's it, Lisa. Stay on a safe subject.

"That's great, Lisa. I'm happy for her. And Mike. But what about you?" His blue eyes pierced hers.

"Honestly, I am not quite sure how to answer that." She pulled a chair next to Scott and sat. "On the one hand, I have confidence that things will work out with my family and my life. I'm truly grateful and thankful for my new relationship with Christ and how it has changed my life. And I'm thankful to you for sharing your faith with me. But am I happy with everything that happened between us this summer? I can't say that I am."

"Lisa, I'm—"

"Scott, wait, please let me finish," Lisa scooted her chair closer and reached for his hand. "I won't lie to you; I came here this summer hoping for a change in our relationship. And when you opened up to me and shared the intimate details of what you'd been through, I thought it might actually be happening." She continued looking intently at Scott. "But what actually happened was God was using all that to open my heart and lead me to Him. I've learned so much about myself this summer. What I need in my life, what that void was, and who could fill it."

"How so?"

"For starters, I know now that it's all about God's love. Listening to your story made me realize the lengths God will go to reach His children. Nothing and no one are beyond His reach. Even when we make mistakes, He remains faithful to us. I know I can't fix all my problems or my parents' problems, but God can. That's part of it, but there is so much more."

Lisa let go of his hand and sat back in her chair. "Over the past few weeks, God revealed two very important things to me. First, He is what I needed all along—a relationship with Him. I was using other things, other people, to try to fill that void that could only be filled by Him."

"Secondly, I'm not ready for a romantic relationship, with you or anyone else. Not right now, anyway. And I'm so thankful to you for not letting me pressure you into something neither of us is ready for."

"Lisa. I'm so glad you understand. I didn't want to hurt you. Your friendship is so important to me, and I've been so afraid I lost that." He smiled. "So we're still friends?"

"Of course we are. We're even better than that," she said, taking both of his hands in hers.

He tilted his head questioningly. "What's better than friends?"

Lisa grinned as a feeling of peace spread through her. "Friends for eternity."

About the Author

Debbie Waltz received a BA in Communication in 2005 at Concordia University and has been writing ever since. Though quadriplegic, Debbie writes intensively, using voice recognition software, and seeks to communicate God's message of faith, hope, and the encouragement of God's unending love. She worked in the disability section of the U.S. State Department for over two years, developing content to support Section 509 training. She has published Christian magazine articles and a chapter in a published book to encourage disabled people.

She gave her life to Jesus Christ and presents a clear description of personal salvation by faith alone and the challenge of pursuing a daily Christian walk for new believers. As a disabled author, she is credible and is *uniquely positioned* to explain the Christian Walk amid life's most serious adversities.

You can find her weekly blog and other writing at DebWaltz.com

You can contact her on Instagram by @rollindebbie or X by @debbiewaltz